CONFESSIONS OF A SIDE B.I.T.C.H.

-His Lies…..

Seazons Collections Publishing House.
603 N.W. 1st Terr.
Deerfield Beach, Fl 33441
Phone: (954) 866-0934

A LETTER FROM THE AUTHOR

Dear readers,

First I would like to thank God for giving me the courage and strength to create this book. A special thanks to Seazons Collections Publishing House for bringing my vision to life. Make sure to purchase my publicist book (Married Man. Twisted Husband). And to my family and friends, thank you for encouraging me to share my story and most of all believing in me.

There are a few of you in particular that I'm hoping this book will really speak to and understand why I chose this title. When I first came up with the story I was very skeptical, because it's a sensitive subject and most people tend not to even talk about. But being that it had hit so close to home I was eager to share so I decided to write about it. The hardest part about this whole journey was my choice of title and rather I wanted to keep it because the word (bitch) just seemed so harsh. In the midst I quickly found out that you can always turn something negative, into something positive. I labeled myself as a bitch which stands for "Brave Individual Telling her Chaotic History. So, it actually turned out perfect .

The thing that inspired me to write this book was, I was once in both women's shoes so I can relate to both situations.

(Being the fiancé /girlfriend) where I had been cheated on lied to, betrayed and just broken completely down by a man that I had given my all. At the time, I started to question and doubt myself thinking I wasn't doing something right, or I wasn't good enough. It took me years to understand that you can be doing everything and it's still not good enough. Leaving out of that relationship I was vulnerable, I was hurt and I was in a very dark place.

When I became the sideline, I had just got out of that ten year relationship with my kids father In the midst I met this man I was naive and I fell into the trap of believing everything he had told me . He was a shoulder to lean on ,he was there for me at my weakest. Come to find out I was only being deceived ,and ended up getting caught up in a worse situation .My biggest regret was not walking away sooner especially after finding out who he really was, although I had so many signs and warnings to walk away I didn't. I allowed my emotions to get the best of me.

God doesn't give us intuitions for nothing if you feel like something isn't right about a person, 9/10 times it isn't right. follow your first mind.

A message for the wives/girlfriends:

A lot of women chose to stay after the pain, hurt and cheating because of marriages or the years they've invested into the relationship but what do you do when you've been betrayed by the person you love. Do you stay? Or do you build yourself up and leave?

A message to the sidelines or other women:

Know your worth! You do deserve better, even after being broken. You don't have to settle. Never play second to anyone. Also Understand that you've played a part in the hurt ,so you have to take accountability as well!

For all ladies I want to say I love you. We are queens and we deserve to be treated just as that . after reading this book, I expect for All women not only to open their eyes but keep them open. There's a blessing behind every lesson.

To the men, I want you guys to understand that playing both sides and chasing your own lust , can leave two women badly scorned (Broken). *Men often underestimate the emotional pain and damage they cause. Having your cake and eating it too is the most selfish thing you can do .*

In conclusion I want to say I'm not perfect. For me this whole ordeal of had put me on an emotional rollercoaster, I nearly lost my mind, my sanity, my religion and everything that I believed in. It took me a while to overcome these obstacles and understand that I was living a lie, he was living a lie and in the end we all lost. Also Not all affairs end well sometimes they can get deadly.

I dedicate this book to my two queens Regena and Ronasia Baker, because if it wasn't from them I would have probably stayed in my mess even longer. As a woman if you have to second guess yourself as to what type of example your setting for your kids that means you're not setting one .

Never Settle you deserve to be treated just as the queens you are!!!

Table of Contents

Confessions of A
Side B.I.T.C.H.

PROLOGUE

"Chris, can you please get out of the mirror? I'm trying to finish my make-up." Brittany groaned.

"And I'm trying to see my abs!" I snapped.

"That's fucking fat! You went to the gym, what? Two times. Now you're fucking Mr. Ebony of the month? Nigga please! Get the fuck out of my mirror and take your ass to work! Bills have to be paid!" Brittany spat.

As much as I wanted to grab her by her throat and choke the shit out of her, I stood there and took every blow. Brittany was my wife. Hell, she was my provider, my shelter, and the mother of my kids. Before marrying her, I was just Chris Kemp. Twenty six years old, working for a valet service making eight dollars an hour. Now, I'm Chris Kemp. Thirty year old, owner of Kemp's Records and Promotions. The hottest record label in Los Angeles, California. My life is like a pretty red rose with one thorn sticking out. The rose is my bank account and lavish lifestyle. That thorn is my wife! After what she just said to me, now I realize why I hate being with her. Hopefully, you'll understand too after you hear my side and where it all started from.

CHAPTER 1

BOOM. BOOM.

The door flew off the hinges. "Chris! Wake up and get the hell out!" Lawrence screamed. He was the building manager and the house nigga for the Landlord. I hated him with a passion.

"Lawrence, I'm not paying for that got damn door! So, when I get my shit and bounce I hope you tell Mr. Chin, you the muthafucker who broke that door down!" I said pointing at the door on the floor.

"Yeah. Yeah. Just get out!" Lawrence hissed.

"I'm going! Let me just grab my shit out the back room! And don't follow me down the hall either. Nigga I don't need an escort!" I barked as I jumped up from the couch and walked to my room. I was sleeping so peacefully until

Incredible Hulk knocked the door down. I thought to myself.

"Chris, hurry up! I don't have all day!" His voice echoed throughout the empty apartment.

"Nigga I'm coming! And where the fuck you have to be?" I barked back as I reentered the living room.

"That's none of your business! Now do you have all your stuff?" He asked.

"All the shit I'm taking! Yeah!" I gritted.

"Good. Now leave!" He ordered pointing his finger towards what use to be the door. As much as I wanted to protest and curse him out, I kept walking. I had a little under thirty minutes before my shift started and I didn't have the time to go back and forth with him.

"Can you at least call me a cab?" I asked.

"You mean to tell me you don't have a phone? Chris, what do you do with your money?" Lawrence sighed.

"Lawrence, that has nothing to do with you! Now can I use your phone or not? I need to get to work!" Lawrence pulled his cell out of his pocket and handed it over to me. I called a cab and returned his phone.

"Are they coming?" He asked.

I nodded my head and slung my book bag over my shoulder. Heading for the nearest exit. By the time I got downstairs, the cab was waiting patiently. I climbed inside and instructed him to take me to the Fountain Bleu hotel three blocks away. Yes, I could've walked, but today wasn't a day to sweat. I feel heated enough. I'm homeless and I'm hungry. And on top of all of that I only have five stank ass dollars in my pocket.

"You've arrived sir." The cab driver announced.

"I see that." I sighed. I handed him the five dollar bill and hopped of the car.

"Chris, you need to move a little faster than what you're doing and clock in. A seminar is being held here today, and the cars are rolling in. So, move it." Chuck instructed.

Chuck was the manager of the lousy company I worked for and a pain in my behind. Although I hated working here, I needed my job. So, I placed my bag in my locker and took my post. The cars were rolling in left and right. Whatever seminar that was taking place had white written all over it. "Lane two, Chris!" Chuck pointed.

I dragged my feet over to the waiting black Bentley coupe and attempted to pull the door open. Surprisingly, the door was locked. The lady behind the wheel sat there speaking into her cell phone staring me up and down. "Well are you going to open the damn door?" I mumbled. It was ninety three degrees and I could feel the sweat beads rolling down my back. Cali was hell in the Summer.

CLICK.

The door latch sounded. As soon as I reached for the door, the young lady shoved it open. "The next time you see someone on a important call, have some respect and stand your ass still until directed otherwise!" The lady spat. I was caught off guard by her tone. A part of me wanted to curse her out but her beauty stopped me. She was a beautiful woman, but only on the outside. She had a kind of understated beauty, perhaps it was because she was so disarmingly unaware of her prettiness. She was beautiful in the classical way with flowing curls. She was shorter than average and certainly larger than a catwalk model, but in her ordinariness she was stunning.

"Can I have your name please?" I asked ignoring her rudeness.

"Brittany Arugula." She stated firmly.

"Ok. Ms. Arugula. Here's your ticket. When you leave stop to that booth over there and we'll be happy to get you your car." I smiled slyly. This bitch had pissed me off but I needed a tip. And from the looks of it, she was carrying more than an American Express card.

"Cute! But I didn't catch your name." She said searching for my name tag.

"Chris." I stated dryly.

"Chris." She smiled gracefully. "I see Chuck didn't quite deliver my message to his employees. So, I'm going to breeze through this once. Just keep up." She stated adjusting her blazer. I was confused. I didn't understand what the hell she was talking about. I looked over at Chuck and he gave me the thumbs up. "Chris, tonight you're going to be my escort inside the seminar. Luckily, I have a stylist waiting on my arrival. She can dress the both of us. Because dear you're going to need it." Brittany looked me up and down as though my attire disgusted her. "You'll get paid five hundred dollars for the hour. All you have to do is escort me in and escort me out. Can you handle that?" She asked.

"Hell yeah!" I grinned. Brittany rolled her eyes.

"Um Chris? It's Chris right?" She squinted her eyes. I nodded my head agreeably. "That language, we don't use unless." She stated.

"Now you can't change the way a nigga talk. I'll escort you in, but this me!" I assured her. Brittany stepped closer to me and leaned in.

"Chris, from the looks of it you can use all the money you can get. So, I suggest you follow me upstairs and make this money." She whispered. The smell of Double Mint rolled off her tongue and up my nostrils. Causing my dick to stand at attention. And that was the day I met Ms. Brittany Arugula.

CHAPTER 2

TWO YEARS LATER

appy birthday baby!" Brittany sang into the air as I rolled over.

"Thank you baby." I replied in a sleepy tone.

"Get up Chris! I have two surprises for you before I go to work!" She said as she crawled on top of me wearing my favorite blush pink teddy.

"What you got daddy?" I said groping her round ass.

"Well, daddy have to get up in order to see! Now come on!" She said tugging at my arm.

"Alright baby. I'm getting up." I surrendered. I pealed the cover back, revealing my naked body. As usual, my soldier stood at attention. "Baby, where did you put my robe?" I asked looking around.

"Oh baby, you don't need it. Just come over here." Excitement covered her face as she motioned me over to our bedroom window that overlooked the front of our estate. "There's your gift." She pointed. A navy blue Rolls Royce was parked near the fountain with a red bow resting on top.

"Babe! I know you didn't!" I shouted. My eyes lit up.

"Yes I did!" She twirled around and wrapped her arms around my waist.

"Damn baby, I don't know what to say." I admitted.

"Well I know what you can say and I know what you could do." She spoke seductively as she twirled her stiletto shaped fingernail across my bare chest.

"Talk to me baby." I ordered.

"First, I want you to make love to me. Then, once you're done I want you to get dressed so we can go downtown and get married." She stated firmly.

"Do you think you're ready to be Mrs. Kemp?" I asked staring down at her. Brittany looked up at me with the biggest smile plastered across her face.

"Yes baby! Yes!" She shouted.

Without further ado, I picked her up off her feet and kissed her passionately. She straddled her legs around my waist as I led her to the bed. Once again, my soldier stood at attention. I gently laid her across the bed and pealed her teddy off her. Those soft perky breast stood firm. Her nipples begged me to suck them. But I wanted to take my time. She had just made me the happiest nigga ever. Buying me a car I only valet parked. So, I was going to give her the loving she'll always remember. Brittany watched as I separated her legs, going head first.

To my surprise she was wearing a see through thong. I pulled them to the side and admired the way her juicy clitoris was jumping. Her well shaved pussy was beautiful. The closer my lips got to Brittany's opening, the louder she moaned. I wanted to tease her a little, so I blew a little air over her vaginal opening. Causing her to shiver. "Ohhhh shit baby. Don't tease me. Suck this pussy!" She begged.

I opened my mouth and went to work. In that split second my tongue caused every nerve in her body and brain

13

to electrify. Brittany gripped the back of my head pushing me deeper into her waterfall as she exploded in my mouth. I could taste the fruit she had eaten the night before. "Baby!" She moaned releasing my head.

"Yes?" I smiled when I looked up and noticed her eyes rolling in the back of her head.

"You never made me feel like that?" She said trying to catch her breath.

"It's always a first time for everything." I winked as I climbed on top of her, easing my thick wood inside her tight opening. After five strokes Brittany began gyrating her hips throwing her pussy at me. "Damn. Slow down." I grunted. Now I was the one trying to keep up.

"Catch this pussy baby!" She yelled out in ecstasy.

"I'm trying..." And just like that, I exploded inside of her. "I could use a nap now baby!" I said climbing off her.

"Oh, no you won't! We need to get dress so we can get down to that courthouse. So, get up!" She said rolling out of the bed.

"Alright baby, get dressed. I'm right behind you."

After many years of being a bachelor, who would have ever thought I would be standing inside a courtroom signing my player card over? Hell, not me. But here I was, standing face to face with a woman I planned on spending the rest of my life with. Mrs. Brittany Kemp. "How do you feel honey?" Brittany shouted looking down at the large rock staring her in the face.

"I feel good baby! I didn't know you had all of this planned already. If I would've known, I would've at least saved enough money to buy you a ring baby. I mean I've been working at the valet service for a few years now and I'm sure Chuck would've given me an advance to buy you one." I said in a sincere tone.

"Honey, I'm sure you would've but the money you make at that valet service isn't enough to buy me the ring I want. So, I took the initiative to buy it myself. And besides, now that we are married you don't have to work!" She said smiling from ear to ear.

"Britt, I'm a man. I must work!" I stated.

"Yeah. But we're wealthy baby. I have more than enough money locked away in oversea accounts and safe deposit boxes. Enough that will be here for our kids and their grandchildren." She explained. I didn't want to seem so anxious, so I remained calm and opened my big ass ears.

"Wealthy?" I asked with raised eyebrows.

"Yes." She giggled. "I hope you don't think I'm buying these fancy cars and living in that big pretty house off my looks?" She continued laughing heartily.

"I didn't say that. But I always wanted to ask." I continued acting innocent.

"Well why didn't you?" She eyed me sideways.

"Britt, that's not my style." I sighed.

"Now that you're my husband, you need to know everything." She paused. I was all ears. I wanted to know. Hell, I got tired of snooping around when she fell asleep anyway. "When I was seven years old both of my parents were killed in a car accident by a drunk driver two months after my father hit the Lotto. After their funeral, family members of all nationalities were saying they were some kin to me. The state wasn't buying it, thank goodness. But after months of being passed around in a foster system, our next door neighbor Ms. Hattie, came and got me. They took her through hell but she won the case. I was thankful for her. She raised me the right way. She gave me knowledge and unlike many Ms. Hattie wasn't after my money. She didn't allow me to touch any of the money my parents left behind until I finished college. Before the death of Ms. Hattie, I opened my business and invested, plus quadrupled my money. And that's the story of my life." Brittany shrugged.

"Damn. I thought I had it rough. But babe, you went through some shit." I scratched my head in disbelief. I had came up with my own assumptions about the way Brittany was living.

"Yes, I've been through turmoil and danced in the rain. But I never allowed it to get me down. That's why when I got to know you and I discovered you were homeless, I took you in. I've been there baby." Her word were sincere and it actually moved me. I reached over and pulled her in close to me. It felt right to kiss her at that moment. Brittany was now

17

my wife and I intended on being with her for the rest of my life. "I see you're trying to finish what you started earlier." She giggled.

"Yes I am Mrs. Kemp." I said sliding my hand up her silicone dress.

"Well that will have to wait because I need to get over to Dedrick office. He's my lawyer. This morning I had him set up a few bank accounts with your name on them and I added your name on the house. He has spare keys to the safe deposit boxes. Anytime you need to access them, all you will need is your identification card." She said with beaming eyes.

"Brittany. Wifey! I don't know what to say." I remained calm. As hard it was to do so, I did. I wanted to kiss her ass right now. I felt like that nigga. A rich nigga!

"Just tell me you love me." She said wrapping her arms around my neck.

"I love you!" I shouted.

We headed over to her lawyers office and just like that, everything was in my possession. I had the keys to everything including her heart. The final surprise was the record label. Without any knowledge Brittany opened it up for me. I didn't know a damn thing about music. But I knew for sure I was going to run it. "How do you feel baby?" She asked as we walked inside our home.

"I feel good B. I mean who would've ever thought, I'll be living like this. Guess God knew what he was doing when he sent you my way. I went from nothing to something over night. I'm still lost for words." I admitted.

"It's nothing baby. And besides you're my husband now. So, we move the same. I can't live a lavish lifestyle and have you out here looking homeless. I don't rock like that." She assured me.

"Thank you baby." I reached over and planted a sloppy kiss on her cheek. Brittany wiggled and giggled trying to get fresh from my grip.

"Chris, stop!" She begged.

"I just love you girl." Now this time I was the one assuring her.

"I know you do. But baby, I need to get in that kitchen and cook. We will play later. I promise." She said breaking free from me.

"Fine." I smacked her backside and followed her into the kitchen.

"Where do you think you're going?" She asked looking back.

"In the kitchen with you." I replied.

"No you're not! Baby, I can manage in the kitchen. I'm sure you've noticed with all these hips and thighs I haven't missed a meal." She joked.

"So, what do you want me to do?" I asked.

"Anything. Take a ride in your new car. Go take a tour of your new record label. Anything! Just stay out of my kitchen." She ordered.

"Ok!" I threw my hands up. "I'll go check things out at the label. I won't be gone long. I love you baby." I kissed her on her full lips and was out the door.

"I use to have nothing. Now I got a whole lot of everything." Jeezy blasted through the speakers of my Rolls Royce as I slid through my old hood. I nodded my head to the beat. I was feeling myself even more now because everyone was on the block. All eyes were on me. When is spotted Tony, I pulled over curbside and hopped out.

"My nigga!" He yelled slapping hands with me.

"What's good?" I grinned.

"You tell me! Looks like your tall black ass done hit the Lotto! Nigga let me hold something!" He said admiring my new ride.

"I'll let you hold something. But I didn't hit the Lotto nigga. So, take your greedy ass on after this." I reached down in my pocket and pulled out a crispy hundred dollar bill.

"Ok bet. Now can you take me to the gas station up the street? I need a cigar and a hot dog." He asked.

"Damn my nigga, do I look like a taxi cab?" I teased.

"Naw. But you look like my nigga!" He laughed. Tony was my best friend. We grew up in the same projects. Growing up we were like peanut butter and jelly. We had to be together. Tony was more than a friend, he was my brother. So, whenever he asked me to do anything I didn't mind. "I like this!" Tony said rubbing the sunroof of the car. "How much did it cost you?" I knew that question was coming next. Tony was cool, but he was also nosey.

"A grip, T. But it didn't cost me a penny. My wife covered the bill." I stated matter of factly.

"Your wife! Nigga when did that happen?" He probed.

"Just a couple hours ago." I said looking down at my watch. Brittany kept me laced in nice jewelry and clothes. The Versace linen collection I was dressed in was even custom made.

"Congratulations nigga. All I'm going to say, she must be special because you Mr. Player, I would have never thought you would've gotten married. I mean all the pussy

you just gave up! My nuts crossing, just thinking about it!"
We both laughed.

"Just don't get that nut juice on my seats nigga." I joked.
We continued laughing and chopping it up until we pulled
up at Sonny's Market and Gas station.

"Do you need something out of here?" He asked
climbing out the car.

"I'm going to grab some gas. But I'll pay at the pump.
Just hurry up my nigga! Don't be in there all day." I ordered.
Although it felt good to splurge around the hood in a
hundred thousand dollar whip, I caught myself missing
Brittany. "Got to hurry up and get back home to wifey." I
mumbled as I stepped out the car. As I began to insert my
new black card into the machine, the sound of clicking heels
grasped my attention.

"Nice car." The woman that those heels belonged to
announced, making her presence known. From her beauty,
she could have graced any billboard or magazine cover.
There was a shyness to her, hesitation in her body
movements and a softness in her voice. Her white dress was

bold against her dark skin, but I could already see her in jeans and a t-shirt to show off her curvaceous frame. There she stood, just feet away wearing a smile that would light up any room. I was like a deer in head lights. I didn't know what to say. I was completely mesmerized.

"Ok." She said in an awkward tone as she turned away in her heels.

"No!" I shouted. "I mean...I'm sorry." I said quickly gaining control of my tone. The young lady stood there staring at me. I know she was calling me every jackass there were. So, I got it together immediately.

"Sorry for what?" She questioned.

"Sorry for being so caught up in your beauty. It was like I heard you talking but I was in a daze." I explained.

"Save your game. I'm sure you have a girlfriend somewhere around here. You look like the type." She fired. In that split second I tucked my hand away behind my back. Remembering the black wedding band wrapped around my finger.

24

"And what type is that?" I smiled slyly.

"You know." She said rolling her eyes.

"Enlightenment." I slid the ring in my back pocket and walked towards her. The closer I got to her, the more the wind blew her perfume in my direction.

"I don't have the time." And just like that her nonchalant demeanor appeared.

"Obviously you do, you've given me this much of your time. So, let's start off the right way. I'm Chris. Chris Kemp." I said extending my hand. She looked down at my hand, searching for a ring.

"Not married." I lied.

"Then my apologies. Cookie." She said shaking my hand.

"Cookie huh?" I asked admiring her from head to toe.

"That's what I said." She smirked.

"Well, Ms. Cookie. May I call you sometimes?" I asked boldly. She sucked her teeth and walked away making her ass bounce like a basketball. With each step she took, my dick started rising.

"555-2367." She said looking back over her shoulder. I grinned from ear to ear. I couldn't wait to call her. I had major plans for that ass. And I wasn't about to foul out.

"How in the fuck did you pull that?" Tony growled.

"It's all game baby." I assured him as we both stood there watching her drive off.

"Game hell. You married now player." Tony's words were like lava. They pierced through my soul, reminding me of Brittany.

"You right." I admitted as I rubbed my beard.

"So, that mean you might as well slide me the number." Tony said with excitement.

"Naw. I can't do that." I said.

"And why the hell not?" Tony's smile flipped upside down.

"Because T, you know me better than that. I'm married at home, but I'm a dog in the park."

CHAPTER 3

When I walked through the door last night, it was much later then I intended. Piles of rose petals led from the foyer of our home to our master bedroom, with a trail of scented candles lighting up the path. Brittany had fallen asleep wearing only yellow boy shorts. I didn't want to wake her because she was sleeping so peacefully. So, instead I eased back downstairs and devoured the plate of food she had waiting for me on the stove's top. In the mix of things, I managed to text Cookie. I didn't expect her to respond being that it was damn near two in the morning. But to my dismay, she responded within seconds. We texted until the sun came up. Talking about any and everything until sleep bags filled my eyes.

"Chris!" Brittany's voice was the alarm I didn't want to hear. I pulled the blanket over my face and rolled over; damn near falling off the couch. "Chris, I know you hear me!" This time she kicked the couch.

"Yes, baby! I do! But I'm sleepy. We'll talk when I get up!" I stated firmly.

"No! We need to talk now!" She kicked the couch again. This time I sat straight up. I rubbed my eyes in attempt of clearing my blurred vision.

After seconds of adjusting my sight, that's when I realized not only was Brittany standing over me with her hand on her hip, but she had my phone dangling in her right hand. "Oh shit!" I thought to myself.

"Do you see this Chris?" She shouted.

"Yes." I answered nervously.

"This is a cellphone! A cellphone that works! A cell phone that should've been in use last night to let me know you weren't coming home right away!" She yelled tossing the phone at me. I stood to my feet and palmed my face in embarrassment. She was right, I should've called. But I'm new to this marriage thing. Less than twenty four hours new.

"You're right baby. I should've called you. It's no excuse. But I was out with Tony. My childhood best friend. We were talking and hanging out at the label. He helped me fix it up a little bit and rearrange the furniture you had delivered. I got so caught up into getting things situated, that I did forget to call. I'm sorry." I spoke sincerely. Brittany dimmed her eyes and smiled slyly.

"I forgive you pookie bear." She wrapped her arms around my neck, and kissed me passionately.

"I love the taste of those." I said in between kisses.

"If you would've been home last night you could've gotten more than a taste of these." She said pulling away from me.

"No baby. Come on! Don't do that. How you come in here starting me up and then pull away when I start rubbing on you? You said you forgive me!" I shouted. Now I was the one yelling.

"I do baby! But just like you have a business to run, so do I. I have to get to the office. I'll see you a little later. Maybe we can do lunch." She said rushing off.

"Lunch?" I frowned.

"Yes! I have to get dressed baby. We can talk over lunch. I love you!" Her voice sounded through the living room's intercom.

"Yea. Ok." I mumbled. I walked back over to the couch and grabbed my phone. Although I felt a shaded vibe from Brittany, I was relieved she didn't go through my phone. Considering, I didn't have a passcode on it. "Close call." I thought to myself as I proceeded into the kitchen. I needed more than a shot of orange juice. I needed a moment to myself to think what the hell had just happened. Excuse me...

***

When Brittany pulled up at the office, she noticed all her employees were in attendance. Even the janitor. That was oddly strange being that at least five people purposely took off everyday throughout the week. "Hmm." Brittany sighed. "I guess everyone needs a full paycheck this week." She spoke sarcastically as she gathered her things to climb out of her Maybach. Brittany ushered inside only to be caught off guard by a surprise of a lifetime.

"SURPRISE!" Everyone shouted.

"What is this?" There was a sweet moment where Brittany's face washed blank with confusion, like her brain cogs couldn't turn fast enough to take in the information from her wide eyes. Every muscle of her body froze before a grin crept onto her face, it soon stretched from one side to the other showing every single tooth. Fresh tulips were everywhere. White balloons danced in every corner of the office. White helium balloons spelled out the words

"Congratulations Mrs. Kemp." Gifts of all sizes were piled on the table near the entrance. And everyone wore a smile.

"Being that you slipped off and got married Ms. Thang without telling any of us, we decided to throw you a office party in celebration of being Mrs. Kemp!" Alicia revealed. Alicia was Brittany's office assistant. She kept things in tact when Brittany was away from the office.

"I don't know what to say? I'm not even sure how you guys found out." Brittany blushed.

"We found out this morning when security found this fine, chocolate brother inside your office a little before midnight, lacing it with every color rose there were. After discovering who he was, security couldn't wait for everyone to arrive! Honey, he told everybody. Including the cleaning staff. So, for those that like to purposely miss work, I called them all and here you have it! We came up with a mini celebration for you honey!" She shouted handing Brittany a champagne glass filled with bubbly.

"Thank you all! I really appreciate it. Yes, I am married and he is one handsome brother! But please get back to work. Money has to be made!" Brittany said adjusting her smile.

"This one rude bitch!" Alicia thought to herself. Alicia produced a fake smile and turned around to face her fellow colleagues. "Well folks, the boss has spoken. Please return to your desks." Alicia spoke firmly. She waited until everyone was out of ear shot then focused her attention back towards Brittany.

"Thank you." Brittany smiled slyly as she began to proceed to her office.

"No big deal. But we need to talk. So, keep marching right on in that office sweetie." Alicia stated matter of factly. When the two of them stepped inside the office, Alicia closed and locked the door behind her.

"You know this is a form of being hostage. Should I scream?" Brittany spoke with much sarcasm as she slumped down in her chair.

"Hostage hell! What is your problem?" Alicia asked.

"What are you talking about Ms. Smith?" She asked in confusion.

"Stop the bullshit Britt. Those employees of yours spent their hard earned money to celebrate what suppose to be a joyous moment, and look how you brushed them off. Do everyday have to be evil ass Brittany day?" Alicia spat. Brittany chuckled loudly. Alicia didn't find anything funny.

"Listen Alicia! I appreciate the gifts and the cheap flowers. But what do you expect me to do? Kiss all their asses.

I think the hell not. I'm running a Publishing company. Not some social call where I sit on my ass and befriend the world. They get paid to work for me. Not accommodate me with balloons and shit!" Brittany spoke harshly. Alicia shook her head. Brittany was a piece of work.

"You need help!" Alicia assured her.

"And you're going to need the unemployment line if you don't get out of my office." Brittany's words were lethal. And her facial expression revealed she was indeed serious. Alicia didn't protest, she gathered herself and left out the same way she came in.

"That little bitch is a piece of work! I can't believe I'm even here putting up with her shit." Alicia mumbled as she made her way back to her desk. It was too early for Brittany's bullshit. So, instead of entertaining Brittany's bitchy ways, Alicia turned on her radio and tuned everyone out for the rest of the morning. She was so caught up in formatting her documents, she didn't even realize someone was standing in front of her.

"Ahem." Alicia looked up from her laptop, discovering a handsome, chocolate, king standing right in front of her.

"Yes? How...how...may I help you?" Alicia stuttered as she finger combed her hair.

"My name is Chris. Is Brittany in here office?" He asked. Alicia looked back over her shoulder and back at him. She climbed out of her chair and made her way around the counter.

"She sure is? But I'm her assistant. I'm Alicia Smith. I pretty much handle everything for her. Contracts, business meetings, as well as personal meetings." Alicia said in a flirtatious manner as she licked her lips seductively. Chris dropped his head and grinned.

"Damn I still got it." He thought to himself. "Alicia, right?" He said looking back up at her.

"Yes." She cooed.

"Alicia, I'm Brittany's husband." Alicia damn near fainted. Her face went from sunshine to midnight. In a split second her happiness was suspended.

"Oh, I'm sorry. I...I...didn't know." She began stuttering again.

"Then next time, ask!" Brittany's unknown presence caught her off guard. Damn near making Alicia jump out of her skin. Chris glanced up and there Brittany were. Leaning against her office door rigid with fury.

"Oh shit." Sweat beads formed across Alicia's forehead. Her palms began sweating. Knowing Brittany as well as she did, she knew she was about to snap. Other employees, wanted to look up from their cubicle. But after seeing Brittany's road of rage on several occasions, they all mind their business and continued working. Chris saw the balls of fire coming in Alicia's direction. So, he interfered.

"Baby, it was innocent. She didn't mean no harm. I should've introduced myself a little better when I walked in. Really!" Chris tried to explain.

"Innocent my ass! Alicia, you're suspended for the remainder of the day. Please leave quietly." Brittany ordered as she began to turn on her heels.

"What?" Alicia shouted.

"You heard me. Now please don't get yourself fired. Be a lady and leave quietly." Brittany stated firmly.

"Fine." Alicia mumbled. She couldn't afford to lose her job. Maybe her dignity, but her job was needed. She had a paralyzed brother and five year old son to take care of and today wasn't the day to lose it all.

"Hmm." Brittany smirked as she continued into her office. Chris was still in disbelief. Brittany had blown things way out of proportion. So, instead of causing a scene, he followed her right into her office.

"Brittany, what that was about?" He frowned.

"What do you think, Chris? No bitch, pretty, ugly, or fine will flirt with what's mine." She stated matter of factly as she wagged her finger in the air.

"But babe, she didn't know." Chris tried to reason. Brittany placed her hands on her curvy hips and looked him up and down.

"I bet she do now!" She gritted. Chris shook his head. He always knew Brittany was a little tough, but not once did he ever think she was cold hearted. "What made you come by anyway?" She questioned as she walked over to her desk.

"Because I was expecting you to call me after you saw the way I decorated your office for you with all these beautiful roses. They reminded me of you, so I had to buy all of them." Chris said looking around as he admired the flowers.

"Cute." She paused. "But they're messing with my allergies. So, please don't do this anymore. As a matter of fact, I'm going to have Rasel throw them out. I don't have time to sneeze and work at the same time." She informed him as she shoved the fresh roses to the side.

"Wow." He whispered as he watched her move around her office as though he wasn't even there. "Brittany, I wasn't aware the flowers would bother you, but please don't throw them out. Give them to someone." He suggested.

"They will not put their paws on these. Waste management will see them instead. I'm texting Rasel now. He'll be up in the next five minutes to dispose them. So, in the meantime I'm going to grab my purse so we can head to lunch." She informed.

Chris was shocked. After revealing his soft side, he was getting pushed over when he usually was the one who did the pushing all his life. "Mama always said a woman that has her own, cannot be told how to act or what to do." He thought as he replayed Brittany's reckless behavior.

"Well are you going to sit in here and grieve about the flowers or are you going to escort me to lunch?" She said rolling her eyes.

"Yeah, B. I'm behind you." Chris mumbled. Brittany's behavior was becoming too intense. He didn't want to address it because he was afraid she would snap on him. So instead, he let bygones be bygones.

"The restaurant I would like to have lunch is on Kirkland's Avenue. Just a few blocks from here. We'll take your car. Head on out and pull the car around front. I'll be out in just a second. I need to use the ladies room." She ordered.

"Ok. See you in a bit." Just as Chris made his way outside, his phone began to dance in his pants pocket. "Who could that be?" He questioned. Text notifications were coming in back to back.

"-Hey Mr. Kemp. Thought of you today. I forgot to send you a contact picture last night. So, here you have it. Take a pick from all three."

Chris lit up with joy when Cookie's face flashed across the screen. "What a beauty." He smiled.

"-Thank you. I'll be sure to decide once I'm done admiring them all." He glanced at the photos one more time then tucked the phone away. He hurried to his car. He didn't want any more of Brittany's rage. In a timely manner, he had his Royce parked right at the door.

"Sorry, I took so long. I had to address an issue before I left." She said as she climbed in the car.

"No problem. You ready?" Chris asked looking over at her. He feared the wrong move would make her flip so he played it her way.

"Yes. And please drive in silence. My head is pounding." She ordered.

Chris didn't mind. The restaurant was just two minutes away. The silence gave him time to think about Cookie and those pictures she had sent him. "We're here." He announced as he pulled up to the valet.

"I can see that." Brittany spoke nonchalantly, helping herself out of the car.

"Would you like to dine inside or out?" She questioned as she fumbled through her bag for her Prada sunglasses.

"I don't want you to work up a sweat. You're already heated enough. So, let's just go inside." He shot back.

"Fine." Brittany shrugged.

Entering the restaurant, Chris noticed how elegant the place actually was. On the outside, it was plain. Just a white building with no windows and little palm trees blossoming on each corner of the entrance. However, inside it was a different appearance. It was a grand space, to say the least. The huge mahogany tables took up most of the vast space.

Two tall, silver candelabras commanded attention from the center of the tables, holding smooth white candles whose wax never dripped.

The lighting was dim and the air was thick with the scents of so many different foods. Chris tried not to gag as a waitress carrying a plate of seafood walked by. He never like the smell of fish.

As they waited to be seated, he listened to the noisy chatter of all the people sitting around while Brittany chatted with the host. "Ma'am your table is ready." A waitress sang walking up to the host stand. "Being that we are a little more crowded than expected, we're going to place you in the booth behind this wall. Please take your seats and a waitress will be over shortly to serve you." She smiled cheerfully as she led them to a private area.

"Baby. Let me get that chair for you." Chris said pulling out the Chiavari chair.

"Thank you." She smiled slyly.

"I'm going to the restroom. If the waiter comes before I get back, just order me something. I'll be back shortly." He said leaning down to kiss her cheek.

"Ok. But no kisses. I'm really not in the mood for that." Brittany rolled her eyes dodging his lips. Chris shook his head in disbelief. Brittany was hard to please and he didn't know if he was the man for the job.

CHAPTER 4

*A*licia couldn't digest the fact that she had gotten suspended. After years of working side by side with Brittany, laughing at her stupid jokes, staying to the office until six in the morning to finish up projects, she had never expected to be the one Brittany shamed in front of the entire staff of employees. So, instead of moping around, she called up her best friend to meet her for lunch. "I can't believe Cruella de Vil did you like that." Cookie shook her head at the thought.

"You can't believe it? Hell, I can. She's an evil bitch. All she cares about is that damn company and making money! I'm still shock the bitch found a husband!" Alicia spat harshly.

"Everybody needs love. Even the meanest people." Cookie said fumbling through her cell phone. Whatever was entertaining her, made her smile from ear to ear.

"Well what have you all over there lightening up like the sun? You haven't even touched your lunch." Alicia pointed out.

"Just texting a friend." Cookie blushed.

"And why haven't I met this friend? He must he ugly!" Alicia teased.

Cookie looked up from her phone with squinted eyes. "Not at all. And if you must know we just started talking. I met him at the gas station yesterday." She explained.

"Oh...I see. So, he must be saying something good. Because you have completely tuned me and your steak out." Alicia smirked.

"I wouldn't dare. But since you think so, I'll just put it away." Cookie said placing the phone on the table.

"Thank you. Now tell me all that you know about him. Maybe hearing about a man will cheer me up. Hell it may even make me have an orgasm!" The girls both chuckled.

"Well if you must know nasty lady, he just opened his own record label, he's single, he doesn't have kids, he drives a bad Rolls Royce and he is fine as hell! Chocolate, tall and handsome. Just like I like them." Cookie sang loudly.

"And he's black?" Alicia joked.

"Yes!" Cookie answered sipping her Long Island Iced tea.

"Damn. Well is his granddaddy looking for a wife?" The girls burst into laughter.

"I'm not sure. He doesn't talk much about his family. Their probably dead or something." Cookie shrugged.

"You know what, on that note it's time to go." Alicia smirked. "What time is it? I better be getting home to Tobias."

"Alicia, when are you going to start living for you? All you do is work, take people's shit, and take care of your family. You need a break." Cookie assured her.

Alicia sighed heavily. "I know Cook. But what else choice I have? My mom isn't here anymore. Usually, it's her running around waiting on every one hand and foot. I guess I took it over. I can't even have a love life because I'm trying so hard to keep my family comfortable. Besides you, their all I have." She admitted.

"I know. So, I tell you what. What if I pay for us to go to Bahamas for a week? We can find a nurse that's willing to stay at the house with Tobias. Make sure he has all his medications on time, eat, and get to therapy daily." Cookie suggested.

"Ok. Sounds good. But what about Torrent?" Alicia asked.

"Torrent can stay at the house with my girls and mom." Cookie stated.

"Hmm. I don't know Cookie. I still have to work. And I don't want to burden anyone with my problems." Alicia hesitated.

"It won't be a burden. Just think about it. Ok?" Alicia nodded her head agreeably.

"I love you heffa." Alicia said leaning over the table to give her friend some love. Alicia and Cookie had been best friends for years. They've experienced each other's hurts and each other's joy. They were more than friends, they were sisters.

"I love you too. Now before we go, let me run to the restroom. Take this and go pay for our meals." Cookie said handing her a few bills. Alicia took the money and Cookie was well on her way to the ladies room.

BEEP. BEEP.

It was the kids. ***"-Mommy, when are you coming home? Daddy stopped by. He said he misses you. Hurry home. Grandma is up dancing again."***

"Just fucking great." Cookie said reading the message over and over. She was so caught up in what her daughters text, that she wasn't even paying attention to where she was going. "Oops! I'm sorry!" Cookie stated as she knelt down to retrieve the contents that fell from her bag. "No, I'm sorry. I should have been paying attention instead of fumbling through this phone."

"No. Trust me. It's fine." Cookie stood to her feet after she collected the last item that was on the floor placing it safely in her purse. "Chris?" Cookie was shocked.

"Oh, wow! Cookie. What are you doing here?" He asked.

"I was having lunch with my best friend. What about you?" She questioned.

"Oh...I'm here with my friend Tony. He's outside on the phone with his girl." Chris lied.

"Oh ok. Did the two of you just get here?"

"Um...no. We about to leave." Chris hesitated as he looked over her shoulder hoping Brittany wasn't no where in sight.

"Alright then. Catch you later." Cookie smiled gracefully and walked passed him. She knew he was watching, so she threw her hips a little harder to make her ass jiggle.

"Got damn! Now that's ass!" Chris shook tremendously. He watched on until Cookie disappeared behind the restroom doors. "I better get my black ass out of here." He whispered walking fast back to Brittany. Approaching the table, he noticed Brittany had company.

"Chris, you remember Alicia right?" Brittany directed her attention over to him. He nodded his head yes. "Alicia was on her way out of the door when she spotted me sipping my Martini. She apologized for her hoe like behavior. And I decided to let her return to work in two weeks." Brittany said with a fond look as she plastered a fake smile across her face.

"Isn't that wonderful." He spoke dryly.

"Very much so." Brittany winked. "Well run along Alicia. Hopefully we won't have this conversation ever again. You're dismissed." She waved her off. Alicia didn't protest. Instead, she walked away without another word. "Cheap bitch." Brittany snarled.

"Brittany, I've lost my appetite. I'm ready to go. Now!" Chris spoke firmly.

Brittany squinted her eyes trying to read his body language. But it was hard. Chris always wore a poker face. She didn't know if she had pissed him off or gotten on his last nerves. She didn't want to test her luck so being the lady she was, she stood quietly. Brittany climbed out of the booth and made her way out of the restaurant wearing the same fake smile she wore daily.

***

Since their arrival home, Chris was anxious to find ways to cheer Brittany up. Being that they didn't get a chance to eat at the restaurant, he came home and prepared dinner. All her favorites. He even called a masseuse service to come out and relax her body. Still, it wasn't good enough. After the hour long massage and pampering, Brittany disappeared upstairs and remained in the bathroom for hours. "Chris, I have a seminar coming up. I have to fly to California tonight. That's what I really wanted to talk to you about." Brittany said peaking her head out of the steamy bathroom.

"Fine time to tell me. Don't you think?" Chris mumbled. Brittany snatched the door completely opened and that's when all hell broke lose.

"What the hell you mean don't I think? Maybe if you put a little effort into running that label, you won't be all in my ass. Go get your own money. Pay a bill around here or something. I've given you the game, now run with it and let me do what the hell I need to do for me!" She snapped.

Chris's entire face flipped upside down. Every word Brittany said had stung. Only fueling the fire that burned inside of him. Every violated word was like gasoline to it. His fists began to clench and his jaw rooted. Burning rage hissed through his body like deathly poison, screeching a demanded release in the form of unwanted violence. It was like a volcano erupting; fury sweeping off him like ferocious waves. The wrath consumed. Engulfing his moralities and destroying the boundaries of loyalty. "Wow." Chris palm his chin. "Brittany before I say the wrong thing, I better get out of here." He spoke calmly. He grabbed his keys off the nightstand then made his way out. Slamming the door behind him.

"Fuck!" Brittany scoffed harshly. "You see what you have done? You made me snap on daddy! Now he's upset. He doesn't even know you're growing inside of me." She gently rubbed the growing baby bump she hid behind the plush towel. Brittany had discovered the morning they got married that she was pregnant. Growing up she always heard:

"Do not bring a child into this world unless you are a married woman."

She didn't want to bring shame upon herself, so she did what she believed was right. "Don't worry your little heart away. As soon as we get back from this trip, mommy promise to make things right with daddy. I'm going to work on my patience and attitude. I just need your help." Brittany massaged her stomach a few seconds longer, then gathered her strength to get dressed. She had less than an hour before her private jet left. "Everything is off and the alarms are set." Brittany gave her home one final glance before retiring into the waiting black Suburban truck.

"Ma'am, you're going to Miami International Airport. Correct?" The driver asked.

"That's what the GPS says." She answered. Brittany retrieved her phone from her bag and dialed Chris's number. As expected, he didn't pick up. "Damn." Was all she could muster up. She tossed the phone back into her bag, pulled her shades over her eyes, then laid her head back on the headrest. Brittany was disappointed in herself. She allowed hormones to spiral out of control. Causing her to lose a great assistant and a once in a lifetime husband.

***

Chris had been riding in circles for damn near two hours. Brittany had called him a dozen times back to back. But he couldn't bring himself to terms to answer her. She had said some lethal words. Words he never thought she would be the one to say. Brittany was his wife. Not just some random street woman. He changed for her. Chris had given up his player ways because he actually cared for her. Even loved her. But his feelings were beginning to change. "Are you going to sit there and dwell on it all night or you going to drive?" Tony called out. Snapping Chris out of his thoughts.

"My bad, T." Chris mumbled looking back in his review mirror. Luckily, no cars were behind him.

"So, check it out." Tony began. "I met a chick over on Blumont this morning. She invited me to hangout with her and a few other chicks. She told me I can bring a few fellas with me. She said they will have food and a little move music going. And it's free. You feeling it?" Tony asked. He was all down for anything that screamed free. Tony was cheap and greedy.

"I don't know, T. I just want to clear my head you know?" Chris explained.

"No, I don't know nigga! Now get your ass off your shoulders and make a left up there on Riverside Drive. You never been like this. You better shake that shit man." Tony schooled. He was right. Chris had never given a woman his heart. He gave out tough love.

"I'm good. Trust me. Now which house it is?" Chris asked scanning the different townhomes on both sides of the road.

"I believe she said 722." Tony shuffled through his memory.

"You believe? Nigga do you know where the fuck we at? I'm not trying to catch a trespassing charge." Chris snapped.

"Man just pull in. That's it right there." He pointed.

"You better hope." Chris eyes him sideways. Just as Tony was getting ready to respond, a light skinned woman, wearing a see through dress came out. Chris looked over at Tony and smiled.

"No panties." Tony grinned. "I told you we was in the right place."

"Then what's taking you so long to get out?" Chris said climbing out the car. Within seconds, him and Tony were on the porch greeting the beauty who came out to take a cigarette break. "Ms. Lady I would love to be the lace on that dress. You are wearing the hell out of it." Tony drooled.

"I'm sure I do. I'm Kesha." She blushed.

"I'm Tony and this Chris. Has the party started?" Tony asked.

"Not without the main course. We've been waiting on dick to arrive all night." She flirted as she licked her lips seductively. Tony's dick jumped up and down.

"Baby, y'all don't have to wait any longer. Because sweet dick Tony is here." He assured her as he tugged at his hard manhood.

"Sounds good to me." She cooed. "Just head on inside. The ladies are waiting. Nivea told us you guys were coming." She said groping his hard on while eyeing Chris.

"I'm going to show you coming as soon as your fine ass get in this house." He smacked her healthy back side and gave her one last wink before letting himself inside.

"It's about time you fools came! We ready to start this card game!" Nivea blurted out.

"Card game?" Tony frowned.

"Ugh...yeah. What else you thought we invited you for?" Kesha said walking up behind them.

"Not no damn card game. Not how you was out there rubbing on a nigga." He hissed. The ladies laughed hysterically.

"Sorry to burst your bubble Tony, but she's gay and I'm fucking her." Nivea smirked.

"Wow." Chris laughed.

"That's alright. I'm going to burst y'all ass in this card game. Shuffle the deck." Tony growled. He pulled up a chair to the table and took his seat.

"Chris, you want to buy in?" Kesha asked.

"No, I'm good. I'm going to chill over here on the couch. Do you mind if I light this up?" He asked holding up his Cuban cigar.

"Well that's not up to us." Nivea assured him. Chris looked around at everyone. He didn't have a clue who to ask. Tony shrugged his shoulders. Chris knew not to ask him. Tony didn't even know who damn house they were even in.

"It's up to me." Chris mouth flew open when the mystery woman came from around the living room corner. Cookie was standing before him in a candy apple red, silicon dress. Her long curly hair flowed down her back. Her freshly pedicured toes complemented the matching sandals. Cookie was stunningly beautiful from head to toe.

"Well may I toke on my cigar beautiful?" He winked. Cookie smiled at the gesture.

"Sure. There's a ashtray next to you. Knock yourself out."

Kesha looked at Nivea and back at Cookie who had made it over to the table. "Um...Cookie, before you sit down can we see you in the kitchen baby?" Kesha questioned.

"Yes. Everything ok?" Cookie frowned.

"Yes. Um...Guys we'll be right back. Make yourselves comfortable. It's food on that table over there and liquor behind the bar." Nivea stated before disappearing into the kitchen.

"Ok. What's the problem ladies?" Cookie asked when Nivea walked in.

"Honey are you blind? That tall, chocolate bar of a man out there looking single as ever and you mean to tell me you don't see him?" Kesha specified.

"Who? Chris? Yes. I've saw him. I know him. But hey, if one of you want him be my guest. I'm good. I've been through enough with these men. You see I'm going through hell with the kids father." She spoke with a sad grimace.

"Listen Cookie, just because that nigga took you through, doesn't mean every man will. Just give it a try." Nivea tried to reason. Cookie released a sight of irritation.

"I'm really not. So can we please return to the card game?" Cookie pleaded.

"Fine. But when your ass end up lonely for the rest of your life, don't call us." Kesha smirked.

"I promise not to." Cookie threw her hands up. Nivea and Kesha brushed passed her to return to their guest.

"Everything ok ladies?" Tony asked.

"Yes. Did you grab yourself a glass of Hennessy, Chris?" Nivea flirtatiously asked while licking her lips.

"I did. Thank you." He nodded. Chris disliked when women threw themselves at him. It was a major turn off. He liked a challenge. And Cookie was the target. However, she wasn't giving he. Chris watched as she sat there playing cards and laughing as though she was the Spades queen. He admired her toughness. Cookie's personality was quite different from her friends and his wife. She was outgoing but humble. And it made him more attracted to her.

"We win Nivea! That's game! Pay the house!" Cookie shouted. Chris sat back and watched them play a round of Spades until the sun came up. "I guess they're right when they say the early birds get the worms. Because Mother Goose got all you bitches money." Cookie chuckled.

"That's alright. I got your ass next time." Kesha said jumping up on her feet.

"Tony baby, maybe you could keep us company. Come take a ride with us. I need my pussy eaten after losing all my money." Nivea assured him. Tony smiled from ear to ear.

"Isn't God is good? My brother. I'll catch you later." Tony grinned as he escorted the two ladies out the door. Chris climbed off the couch and on his feet.

"Well, I guess that leaves the two of us. Would you like a hand cleaning up?" Chris asked.

"No. I think I have it. Thank you." Cookie said walking towards the door.

"Oh. Ok. Well can I call you later. Once you wake up?" He asked trying his luck.

"Um...I don't know. If I have time, I'll call you." She lied.

"Ok. I'll be waiting." He smiled. Cookie waited until he was out the door then she released the deep breath she was holding.

"Thank goodness he is gone. That man made my soul shake." She mumbled. Although, Kesha and Nivea felt she needed someone, Cookie felt different. She wanted love but she wanted the right love. And she wasn't ready to rush things.

CHAPTER 5

"M rs. Kemp it looks like you're ten weeks pregnant. This little munchkin is growing fast. On our last visit, you were just four weeks." Dr. Wihcon acknowledged as he printed out the sonogram.

"Yes, this little baby is growing pretty fast. So fast, I haven't even mentioned it to my husband yet." Brittany sighed heavily. Dr. Wihcon looked up from his laptop. He could see the stress upon Brittany's face. He could hear the agony in her voice.

"Wait. I thought you promised to tell him when I came over to California to visit you?" The wrinkles in his forehead pronounced.

"I was but I couldn't get enough courage to do so. Every time we communicate, I lash out at him. We can't even hold a decent conversation without me wanting to take his head off." She admitted.

Dr. Wihcon gave a chortle. "Brittany, I don't mean to laugh dear but that's natural. Those are your hormones. Being that this is your very first pregnancy, I know you wouldn't understand. So, I'm going to prescribe you some medication that will help you relax more." Brittany flinched.

"Don't worry, it won't hurt the baby. Relax. Ok?" Brittany nodded her head agreeably. She trusted Dr. Wihcon. He had been her OBGYN since she first discovered she needed one.

Two years ago, he moved from California. Traveling down to the South shores. Brittany was disappointed when he left. He was the only gynecologist she trusted. So, instead of finding another one in her state she agreed to travel away for each doctor's appointment. "Here you go Mrs. Kemp. You're all set." Dr. Wihcon said handing her a bag full of goodies. "Everything you may need is inside. Even the pregnancy do's and don'ts. Trust me, after this first trimester it won't be as bad. Get home to your husband and talk to him." Dr. Wihcon ordered as he helped Brittany out of the recliner. He led her back to the main lobby, turning her over to her driver. He waited until she was well tucked in the backseat before waving goodbye.

"Are you ready Mrs. Kemp?" The driver asked.

"Yes. I am." She paused. "Are you ready to go home to surprise daddy?" She asked rubbing her belly. "He's going to be so excited to hear how you're growing inside. But in the meantime, I better take one of these to relax me before we arrive." She grabbed a bottle of water out of her bag then tossed the tablets back. She leaned her head back on the headrest, allowing the pills to take it's course.

***

Evening had come and Cookie's day had just begun. When everyone left her house early that morning, she crawled in bed and slept like a log. "So, you mean to tell me you're just getting up?" Alicia asked.

"Yes for the hundredth time.!" Cookie said in a agitated tone. "The kids are with their father. And I told you I was having a gathering at the house last night. We end up playing cards until the sun rose." She explained.

"I started to come. But I couldn't find a sitter for Torrent." Alicia explained.

"It was nice. Kesha and Nivea came over. They didn't tell me they were inviting two guys though." Cookie rolled her eyes.

"Child please. You know how those heffas get down. Surprise they didn't leave with one of them." Alicia joked.

"Don't speak so fast." Cookie warned.

"Girl I knew it! Just a bunch of hoes." Alicia shouted.

"Them hoes are your cousins. Don't forget." Cookie laughed.

"Don't remind me. But why didn't they take both men? I know they probably wanted to." Alicia sucked her teeth.

"Actually, you wouldn't believe who the second guest was." Cookie snarled.

"Who?" Alicia questioned.

"You remember the guy I told you about when we were having lunch?"

"Yea. The one with the Royce." Alicia recalled.

"Well the guy that Nieva and Kesha left with, my friend and him are good friends." Cookie explained.

"Girl, no!" Alicia hissed.

"Yes. Small world." Cookie smirked.

"Well honey, don't let them get anywhere near him if you're trying to keep him. The heffas will suck him dry." Alicia stated matter of factly.

"You know what, on that note I'm ending the call. Bye Alicia." Cookie disconnected the call. "That girl is crazy." She laughed. She gathered her purse and headed out. As she was locking her door, a large hand rested on her shoulder. Causing her to damn near jump out of her skin. "Chris!" Cookie shouted when she caught a glimpse of his face. "What are you doing here?" She asked.

"I'm sorry if I startled you. I just wanted to see you. Last night you were so distant as though I did something to you. From the text messaging back and forth, I figured there was some sort of connection between the two of us." He explained. Cookie tossed her purse strap over her shoulder and looked directly in his eyes.

"Listen Chris, you seem like a very nice person. You really do. But I'm not trying to give my heart to anyone at the moment. I just recently got out of a long term relationship with my kids father, and that was a rollercoaster of it's own. So, please understand." She tried to reason.

"As beautiful as you are Ms. Cookie, that's hard to even do. I understand the way you feel about men and relationships, but they're not all the same." He assured. Cookie bit down on her bottom lip. She was feeling Chris but she was afraid of a guy of his statue.

"Well I don't have time to find out. So if you'll excuse me, I have to get to the gym." She said tugging at her car's door handle. Chris smirked.

"Well I guess you won't see the gym today because I'm not moving my car until you give me a chance." He shrugged. Cookie placed her hand over her face.

"You can't be serious?"

"Watch me." He winked as he walked to the back of his car. He popped his trunk and pulled out what looked like red picnic blanket.

"What are you doing, Chris?" Cookie questioned.

"Hmm. Just getting comfortable. Looks like we may be out here all night at the route you're going. So, I better wrap up. I don't have any mosquito repellent, so this should keep them off for now." He said leaning against his car.

"Unbelievable." Cookie blushed. "Chris, you know this isn't right. I paid my personal trainer for the day. And if I miss the day, that money is nonrefundable." She smacked her lips.

"Ok. How much was it." He reached in his pocket and pulled out a wad of bills. Cookie looked down at the roll and laughed.

"Cute! But Chris, I can definitely handle my own. A roll of hundreds, fifties, or twenties impress a woman that gets her own." She stated matter of factly.

"Hmm." Chris shoved the money back into his pocket.

"Hmm what?" Cookie demanded to know.

"You just made me want you more." He grinned.

"Oh my goodness." Cookie whined. Chris thought it was funny. He stood there with the biggest smile upon his face.

"All you have to do is give me a chance. One week. If I disappoint you within that week, I won't say another word. But if you don't give me a chance, I guarantee you I'll be here in your driveway every day singing to the top of my lungs. With a live band in the road. Literally." The look in his eyes assured Cookie he was pretty much serious.

She dropped her head, releasing a heavy sigh. "Fine! One week! But I guarantee you, neither of us wouldn't like it!" She groaned.

"Only time will tell." He flashed his million dollar smile. He knew he had Cookie exactly where he wanted her.

"Ok, you got what you want. Now can you let me out?" She pleaded. Chris wagged his finger in the air.

"No dear. You said a week. And that week starts now. You're mine. So, please climb into the passenger seat. We have a ice cream parlor that's waiting on our arrival." Cookie took a two steps then hesitated for a moment. She looked back at him and Chris had the silliest look on his face.

"One week." He reminded her. She gave him a warm smile then climbed into the passenger side of his car. "Never been in one of these before." Cookie pointed out as she examined the interior features of the Rolls.

"It's a lot of things you'll experience that you've never have after this long week." He winked.

"Is that so?" Cookie blushed.

"Yes ma'am. Starting with this place we're turning in." He nodded.

"I thought we were going to the ice cream parlor?" Cookie frowned.

"Can you allow me to do me?" Chris placed his hand over his chest. Cookie laughed at his body language. "Fine. Be my guest." Cookie surrendered.

"First, I'm going to need you to place these over your eyes." He directed as he pulled a silky scarf from his glove department.

"Boy. Is you..." Chris threw his finger in the air cutting her or mid sentence.

"I lead. You follow. Now close your eyes." He placed the scarf over her eyes then led her up the spiral staircase.

"Chris, I don't know about this." She groaned.

"Relax. We're almost inside. Step up." He instructed. He opened the door and led her in the office of his record label. "What do you think?" Chris asked unraveling the silk scarf. Cookie looked around admiring the showcase that consisted of different ice cream flavors. Behind the showcase stood a male server.

"I'm speechless." Cookie breathed.

"And you should be. Luckily I was able to book Simon here at the last minute. He's always busy. I guess that's why I put so much effort in getting you here." He winked.

Cookie tried to hide her smile. But the feeling felt too good to do so.

"You're something else Chris."

"I believe I am Ms. Cookie." He grabbed two spoons and a large container off the top of the showcase and the two of them devoured every flavor ice cream there were. After getting a tummy full, they sat and talked about everything they could think of. Chris even handed Cookie a microphone to show off her vocal skills in the booth. Things were starting to unwind unexpectedly.

***

"Welcome to Kemps Records And Promotions." Tony shouted.

"You must be Tony." Brittany pointed out. She remembered him from the picture Chris kept in his nightstand.

"Yes. And you must be the beautiful Mrs. Kemp. My brother has told me so much about you. The pictures he showed me of you, doesn't do any justice." Tony smiled nervously.

"Well thank you Tony. Is my husband inside?" Brittany asked.

"Umm. I actually just got back to my desk. Let me call his desk phone just to be sure."

"Oh. There's no need. He'll love the surprise being that I just touched back down from my trip." She assured him.

"Trip? Girl where were you?" Tony pried.

"I traveled South. Chris didn't tell you?" She frowned.

"He probably did. But it slipped my mind. I smoke so damn much." Tony explained as he quickly sent Chris a text.

"Ok. Well it was nice chatting with you, Tony. See you when I come out." Brittany smiled.

"Wait!" Tony paused. Stopping Brittany in her tracks.

"Yes." She turned around swiftly.

"Do you have a sister?" He asked.

"No. I'm the only child." She noted.

"What about a auntie?" He scratched his head.

"No. Not at all." Brittany frowned.

"Your grandma still living? I know your granddaddy Viagra no longer kicking in." He winked.

"Eww Tony that's disgusting!" She shouted.

"Very much so." Chris interrupted.

"My bad brother. Just trying to get my foot in the door." He said adjusting his crouch.

"Sorry about that baby." Chris said directing his attention towards Brittany.

"That's fine. I've been here for about ten minutes now. I started in the back but as you could see I got boxed in by your receptionist." Brittany eyed.

"I'm sorry baby. When did you get back in?" He questioned.

"A little over an hour ago. I went home first. Didn't see you. Figured you were here. How's things coming along?" She questioned.

"Um...Pretty good. I actually was working on a project before you got here." He stated.

"That's great baby. I'll love to hear all about it when I come out of the restroom." She said. Brittany reached up and kissed his cheek then hurried off to the ladies room.

"You better hurry up and get that chick out the back. I'll stall. Just go clear that room." Tony whispered. Chris marched back to his office as fast as he could. Cookie was still in the booth playing on the mic.

"Cookie, can you step out for a minute?" His voice sounded over the intercom. Cookie came out wearing the biggest smile ever.

"Yes."

"I know you're in there enjoying yourself. But it slipped my mind that one of my artist had studio time today. She's waiting for me in the lobby. Do you mind if Tony take you home while I handle this business. I promise to stop by later if you're up to you." He pleaded.

"Oh. Sure. No problem. I really enjoyed myself by the way." Cookie smiled.

"My pleasure." Just as he were escorting her out, Brittany was letting herself in.

"Hello." Cookie's perky voice sounded.

"Hi." Brittany spoke dryly.

"B, this is the project I mentioned earlier. The voice she has is amazing. Thinking about letting her join the team. I was just in the office telling her about you." He lied.

"Is that right?" Brittany smiled gracefully.

"Yes. He actually did. And it's a honor meeting someone who work so hard. People truly don't understand. But us black girls rock." Cookie winked. Tony burst into laughter causing everyone to look in his direction.

"Something funny, T?" Chris squinted his eyes.

"Oh. No!" He said.

"Ms. Lady, you ready to ride?" Tony cleared his throat.

"Yes. Again, thanks Chris. I really enjoyed everything. And it was nice meeting you too." Cookie delivered one last smile before making her way out.

"Alrighty then! That went well." Brittany spoke.

"Thank God." Chris thought.

"So, baby I'm so happy that we are alone. It's something I need to tell you." She grinned.

"And what's that babe?" Chris asked.

"Well...I'm pregnant!" She shouted.

BOOM.

Chris dropped the microphone that he had in his hand. "Chris, is everything ok?" Brittany questioned as she examined his blank stare. She didn't know what to expect. Chris looked as though he had saw a ghost.

"Yes...Wow...How many days are you?" He whispered.

"Days?" Brittany shouted.

"Chris! I'm ten weeks!" She noted.

"Wow." He breathed. Brittany placed her hands on her hips. Her left foot tapped away at the floor.

"Please tell me wow means your happy?"

"Of course babe. Just speechless. Come over here." Chris grabbed her by her waist, pulling her close to him.

"I love you Mr. Kemp." Brittany sang.

"Me too." He mouthed hugging her as tight as he could.

"Damn, I'm not ready for this." He thought to himself as he closed his eyes.

CHAPTER 6

It had been a week since Cookie last saw Chris. He wasn't responding to her texts or calls. The other day when Tony drove her home from the label, she called him several times. She had misplaced her house keys and wasn't sure if they had fallen out in his car or if they were left in the studio. But to her dismay, he didn't answer. Luckily, she kept a spare under the flower pot. However, she was stuck in the house because her car key was on the missing keychain. "I better clean this house up before these clients of mine start pouring in." She mumbled. Cookie was a hairstylist. The best one in town. Some of her regular customers flew in twice out the month from different states just to have her special touch. Cookie was a master when it came to the flat iron and comb. She hoped and dreamed of one day opening her very own salon. That was her dream since she was old enough to understand.

"Aren't you a beauty?" Chris said sneaking up behind Cookie locking his arms around her. He had caught her completely off guard.

"Chris. Stop! Let me go!" She wiggled trying to release herself from his grip. "And what are you doing here? And how did you get in my house?" She barked.

"That's the way you talk to your man?" Chris asked sarcastically.

"You're not my man! Now answer me!" She shouted.

"Ok. Ok. Calm down tiger. When I knocked on the door, you didn't come to the door. I figured you was upstairs and couldn't hear my taps. I knew you were inside because your car was parked outside. So, after a few more knocks, I tried my luck to twist the knob. Surprisingly, the door was unlocked." He explained.

"Wow. I could've sworn I had locked that door. I never leave me door open. That's strange. Anyone could've came in here and killed me or burglarized my home." She whispered frantically.

"Yes. You have to be careful babe." He applied the bullshit on thick. Truth be told, Cookie left her keys on his desk at the studio. When he convinced her to go in the booth and play on the mic, he took her keys, hiding them. After making sure Brittany got home safe and tucked in, he went out and had keys copied from the original key. Keys to Cookie's house, mailbox, car, and he even made a copy of the two other mystery keys that was on her chain.

"You're right. But honestly Chris why haven't you returned my calls or texts? I've been stuck in this house for days. Unable to move my car. Thankfully, all my clients are able to come to me. I've would've lost out on serious loot if it was the other way around." She admitted.

"Those clients...are they all females?" He questioned with a serious look.

"No." Cookie giggled. "Ladies aren't the only ones who gets their hair done. I have eight male clients." She pointed out. Chris's entire facial expression change.

"You know people are crazy these days. They will try to take advantage of you. You should stop doing those guys hair and stop allowing them to come here." He stated firmly.

"No. They're cool. I've been doing each one of their hair for years." Cookie assured him.

"You won't be doing their hair any longer." He thought to himself. "Yeah. Well what are your plans for the day?" He asked switching the conversation.

"Um...I have one client that should be here in the next 30 minutes." She said looking down at her watch. "She's just getting a touch up."

"Ok. So after she leave, I want you to hurry upstairs so that you could get dress. I'm taking you out tonight." He winked as he turned to escort himself upstairs.

"Whoa." She said shaking her head.

"What's the problem?" He asked with squinted eyes.

"You! You're the problem! You come here asking for a chance. Then you get missing for days. No calls or anything. But you expect me to fall in your arms and you can't even

84

give me a explanation. Wow!" Cookie rolled her eyes in disgust. Chris took a few steps back towards her and gazed into her eyes.

"If you must know, my only living relative passed away. My cousin. I couldn't get myself together mentally. So, I've been at the label praying and listening to music to clear my mind." He lied. In that moment, all Cookie's anger went out the window. Her heart felt much sympathy. She thought she could feel the pain he was feeling. But she wasn't sure.

"Chris, I'm so sorry. Is there anything I can do?" She asked sympathetically.

"I don't know. I just don't want to be alone." Chris continued applying the bullshit on thick.

"I tell you what...how about I cancel my appointments and we go out somewhere. Maybe a movie or dinner. Somewhere in town. What do you say?" She asked. Chris frowned and shook his head disagreeably.

"No. I'm good. I don't want to be out amongst people. I rather stay here and chill or just go back to the label." He continued lying. The truth was he didn't want to be seen in public with another woman. Brittany was well known and he didn't want to risk it.

"Ok. Cool. Just give me a minute to cancel the appointment and we can catch a Netflix." She noted.

"Sounds good. I'll be upstairs. I just need to lay down. My head is pounding." He pointed out.

"Ok. I'll be up soon. I just need to cancel her appointment on the application on my computer." She said retrieving the MacBook from off the counter. "By the way, my room is the one straight ahead as soon as you get to the top of the stairs." She called out.

While Cookie made preparations to cancel her client's appointment, Chris had other plans. "Looks like you will be getting blocked Mr. Thompkins and so will you Devin." He smirked devilishly as he scrolled down her contact list. Cookie had left her unlocked iPhone on her nightstand, accessible. Chris blocked every male number in the phone and even browsed through Cookie's text messages. "Who in the hell is this clown?" Chris mumbled as he came across her kids father rude text thread.

"Chris! I'm coming inside and I have something to cheer you up." Cookie sang as she made her way up the staircase. Chris quickly placed the phone back on the nightstand and laid back on the bed as though he was sound asleep. "Chris?" She whispered.

"Yeah." He answered in a put together sleepy tone.

"I didn't mean to wake you. I thought maybe you were still up." She explained.

"I thought so too. I must have dozed off." He said sitting up rubbing his eyes.

"I see. I bought you a tray of fruit and crackers, some cranberry juice and a bottle of water." Cookie placed the tray down next to him.

"Aww. Thanks." He smiled.

"No big deal. So, what do you want to watch? A thriller, romance, or drama?" She said retrieving the remote off the dresser.

"Honestly, I prefer watching you." He flirted. Cookie blushed. She didn't expect to hear that.

"Besides me." She said clearing her throat.

"Anything." Cookie scrolled through the channels until Tyler Perry's "Meet The Brown's" stopped her in her tracks. "Great selection." Chris complimented.

"Tell me about it. I can watch Tyler's movies and plays all day." She assured him.

"Well come get comfortable. Just because I'm in your bed doesn't mean you have to be a stranger to your pillow." He said tapping the empty space next to him.

"No. I'm fine right here."

"Please. I don't bite." He begged. Cookie hesitated for a second then gave in. Chris's puppy dog eyes moved her. She removed her slippers and climbed right next to him. The two sat up enjoying movie after movie until they both dozed off.

RING. RING.

Chris's cell sounded. It was a text from Brittany. Chris looked over at a sleeping Cookie and eased himself up out of the bed. He crept out of Cookie's bedroom heading straight down the stairs. When he reached the bottom step he looked over his shoulder one last time, making sure Cookie didn't awaken. Realizing the coast was clear, he proceeded to Cookie's out door balcony to call his beloved wife. "Hey baby." He sang into the phone placing it on speaker.

"Hey back." Brittany's bubbly voice sounded.

"What are you and my sweet bundle of joy doing?" He asked in a level tone.

"We just finished up our bubble bath. We were calling to see what time we should be expecting you home tonight." She replied.

"Well, I'm driving down the coast with Tony. He has discovered me some new talent. He let me listen to her demo and baby, she's gifted. I couldn't turn down this offer. But I will be home before noon. Just try to get some rest for me and send me some naked pictures. You know I'm in love with your body." He lied.

"Oh ok baby. I guess I'll turn the oven off and put the food up. Drive safe. I love you." She sang proudly.

"I love you too." Chris disconnected the call and slid the phone into his right pocket.

"Who do you love?" Cookie asked in a settled tone. Chris damn near jumped out of his skin. But he didn't show any sign of being startled or guilty.

"My neighbor. Ms. Maggie. She's keeping an eye on my house for me. She has this very big thing when it comes to the word love. So, before ending each call she always says it." He smiled.

"Hmm. Ok." Cookie smirked.

"She's cute as a button. I would love for you to meet her soon. She can be a grouchy old lady, but she's lovable. I look at her as my wealthy grandma." He laughed. Chris lies were starting to pile up. And he prayed none of them revealed. But as promised...what's done in the dark, will eventually come to the light.

"So, being that we slept the day away, what are your plans for the night? Netflix and chill isn't for either of us." Cookie assured him.

"Especially not you. Babe, you were snoring and slobbering." He joked.

"I was not!" She burst into laughter.

"You were babe. The walls even shook a few times. Thank goodness your neighbors didn't call the police." He said shaking his head.

"Oh stop it! I never snore." She giggled.

"I'm telling you. And here's the proof. You have crust on the side of your mouth." Chris said wiping the crumbs free from the corner of her lips. Before Cookie could say thank you, he leaned in and stole a kiss.

"What are you doing?" She breathed.

"Something I wanted to do since I've laid eyes on you." He said in between kisses.

"No. Chris. We can't." She whispered trying to break free from his grip. Chris ignored her and proceeded kissing her passionately. He tighten his grip around her waist. Cookie's Vanilla scent ran through his nose causing his toes to tingle.

"You can plead rape, and I'll plead guilty. But Cookie I can't stop. I haven't stop thinking about you since the day I've laid eyes on you. I couldn't wait for this moment to present itself." He explained as he rubbed her apple behind.

"Chris, you barely know me." Cookie whispered.

"I will after this." Chris scooped Cookie off her feet and carried her up the staircase. He placed her down on the pillow top bed and smile at the beautiful view before his eyes. Cookie flinched when Chris reached out to touch her. "It's ok." He whispered. He unbuttoned her dress and began kissing her stomach slowly. Cookie's chest heaved up and down. "Relax." He coached. When Cookie felt Chris's warm tongue trail her stomach, she jumped. Chris's thick warm tongue felt good in a strange way. "Are you ok?" He asked. Cookie nodded her head agreeably. "I'm going to remove your panties using only my teeth. I promise not to bite." He winked. As stated he locked his teeth into her black boy shorts. Tugging them to her ankles. He then lifted her left foot into the air, placing her pedicured toes close to his mouth. Cookie damn near fainted when she felt his warm breath brush against her skin. Chris licked her toes in a swift manner.

"Ooh." Cookie moaned.

"Come here." He ordered. He grabbed her by the hand, pulling her up close against his chest. His hand gently glided through her hair, as he looked at her in a way he had never looked at his wife or any other woman before. Her eyes were candles in that night. "You're beautiful." He complimented. As a small but teasing smile crept upon her face, goosebumps lined her skin, not the kind than one gets in the cold, but the kind one gets when nothing else matters except right here, right now. Chris retrieved a condom from his pocket and placed it on his hard manhood. Cookie watched on as he rubbed his shaft up and down. "You're ready?" He asked.

"If I say no, what would it matter to you?" She shot back.

"It wouldn't." He admitted. He reached behind her and unlatched her lace bra revealing her milky breasts. Her enlarged brown nipples dotted both her breasts. "Show time." He grinned. He laid Cookie on her back then the fireworks exploded. Entering Cookie wasn't easy. He could tell Cookie hadn't slept with another man in a while. With each stroke, her body tighten and she moaned louder. The louder she got the harder he thrust. "Damn baby, this pussy good." He groaned. Chris imagine taking his time, but as good as her pussy was, he was about to nut. "Baby, we have to slow it down or daddy's going to cum." He grunted.

"Not...yet." Cookie cooed. Her eyes began rolling back and her hips gyrated in circles.

"Fuck Cookie!" Sweat beads formed across his forehead. Cookie was taking him on a ride of his life and the crazy part about it, he was the one on top. "Baby, this pussy wet. Damn it feels like a waterfall." Chris moaned. "Damn! Marry me!" When those words left his lips, it was no turning back. Cookie threw her pussy like a pitcher would throw a ball. "Fuuuccckkkk!" He hissed. Cookie had rocked his world. And for the first time in life, he had tapped out.

GIGGLES

"What's funny?" Chris asked.

"You. All that noise you was talking and look at you."
She laughed. Chris legs was shaking. He couldn't keep up.
When he thought he was going to put it on her, she had put
it on him.

"Ha. Ha. Come here." He ordered. Cookie grabbed her
robe off the chair and placed it around her. She walked over
to him and stood directly in front of him. "How do you
feel?" He asked looking up at her.

"I'm ok." She shrugged.

"Just ok?" He smirked.

"I'm fine." She assured.

"I don't want you to feel as though you was force to do
something you wasn't ready for. I know it may seem as
though we rushed things, but Cookie from the very first day
I saw you, I knew I wanted to have a future with you. And
we're grown. We both know what we want. I don't expect
you to fall in love with me by morning, but want you to
place your trust in me and know that one day I'm going to
make you the happiest woman there is." He paused. "I want
so much for you. I want to help you get a salon and let you

do what you do best. I want to help you build a empire so you won't have to worry about another man. I want to be that man for you. Just trust me. If we have trust, we can go a long way. You're the only woman I need and the only woman I believe is for me. Just trust me." He begged. Cookie released the deep breath she was holding and looked into his deep dark eyes.

"I'm afraid." She whispered.

"It's ok to be afraid but I'll never hurt you. Just trust me." He pleaded.

"Ok. I trust you. But if it's anything I need to know, please tell me now." She tried to reason. Chris stood to his feet and placed her hands on his chest.

"Baby, there's nothing more you need to know. Just understand I'm going to make you're happy." He smiled. Cookie wrapped her arms around his neck and kissed him long and hard.

CHAPTER 7

SIX MONTHS LATER

Looks like you got your wish young man. It's a boy!" Dr. Wihcon grinned.

"Thank you, Doc! Thank you!" Chris smiled from ear to ear. He was proud to shake Dr. Wihcon's hand. Chris always dreamed of having a house full of boys. He wanted his own football team. Chris had a daughter name Christina. She was ten years old. Christina lived in Florida with her mom. Chris never got a chance to see her now that he was with Brittany. Hell, Brittany didn't even know Christina existed. He didn't know how she would have accepted it. So, he never mentioned it.

"What's on your mind baby?" Brittany asked interrupting his thoughts.

"Oh. Nothing! I'm happy. Very happy! That's all." He smiled.

"I'm happy too. Can't wait for this little fella to arrive. He's causing this waist of mine to expand drastically." Brittany groaned.

"You're fine baby. You should be thankful. My little man has given you some more hips and thighs." He winked.

"Baby, stop it. I know you think I'm a whale." She whined.

"I sure do. Now let's swim home Shamu." He teased.

"I got your Shamu! Bet Shamu won't be backing it up for you tonight." She eyed him sideways.

"Babe, I was joking." He laughed.

"Ha. Ha. Hell." She shot back.

"You know I love you girl. Now give me those lips." Brittany reluctantly gave in.

"Babe, what are our plans tonight?" She asked as he escorted her to the car.

"As soon as you climb into that seat, I'll tell you." Chris said holding the door open for her. After tucking herself safely in, he walked around to the driver side and climbed in.

"I'm all ears." She smiled.

"So, when we get home, I'll lead you into the kitchen. Where a chef is already in place preparing all your favorite foods. After you partake in enough dinner and dessert, I'll carry you up stairs and run you a hot bubble bath. I will wash your body top to bottom. Then I'm going to make sweet love to you until you can't take anymore. And finally, we will fall asleep in each other's arms until it's time for me to wake up and plan another beautiful day all over again." He winked.

"Baby! I love you so much!" Brittany shouted as she danced in her seat. She was anxious to get home. Chris had her panties soaked. "I'm going to give it to you baby." She promised.

"I want you to." He licked his lips seductively.

"Then drive!" Brittany whined.

"I'm driving baby." He assured.

Chris took the expressway back to their house in a timely manner. He assisted Brittany out of the car, and into the house. As promised, a chef cooked dinner, Brittany stuffed her face, and Chris ran her a hot bath. However, by the time he laid her in bed, she was out like a light. So, the making love and cuddling was out the window. "Thank God." He thought to himself. "It's hard juggling good dick back and forth. God knows I couldn't do it tonight. This sweet thing belongs to Cookie tonight." He smiled at his own thoughts. Chris kissed a sleeping Brittany and quickly redressed himself. Within minutes, he was out the door and headed for Cookie.

***

"I haven't heard from you Ms. Thang." Cookie sang into the phone.

"I know. I started back working. So, I've been extremely busy these past couple months. This boss lady of mine has had me on my toes. She even has me working seven days a week now." Alicia spat.

"Damn! That's crazy!" Cookie shook her head.

"Tell me about it. But hey I'm dealing with it." She assured her.

"So, what's new with you?" Alicia asked.

"Well, if you should know my new boo and I have made things official." She sang.

"Child, no!"

"Yes!" Cookie shouted.

"He's been so sweet and charming. It's nothing I can't ask for that he hasn't given me. Tonight I'm cooking dinner for him and after, we're suppose to go for a walk a beach." Cookie stated.

"Where's the kids?" Alicia questioned.

"With their father. He came and picked them up last night." She noted.

"Cool. So, tell me this. How does the girls feel about him?" Alicia asked.

"They love him and that's what makes me love him. He's so good with them. He buys them any and everything. Being that he doesn't have kids, he's so attached to them. And I love it all." Cookie explained.

"Well, I'm happy for you. You deserve it all. You've been through enough. So, accept God's blessings honey. Who knows, he may be your husband." Alicia pointed out.

"Only time will tell." Cookie sang.

"It sure will." Alicia agreed.

"But Alicia I really miss your ugly butt. And I was thinking before you go home, you should stop by. Just for a hug or something. I mean dang! Give me that at least!" Cookie smacked her teeth.

"Say no more! Are you home now?" She asked.

"Yes I am. Now, are you coming!" She shouted.

"Yes. I'll be there in two minutes. Unlock the door scrub." Alicia teased.

Cookie disconnected the call and climbed off the couch to greet Alicia at the door. She was excited to have her friend over. They hadn't kicked it in months. Whenever they were apart for months at a time, Cookie didn't feel right. "Aww. The baby missed me that much, she had to greet me at the door?" Alicia teased.

"Shut up and hug me! Heffa!" Cookie grabbed her friend and held her tight. She felt better knowing Alicia was in her presence.

"So, what's for dinner? Because I'm hungry!" Alicia inquired.

"And who said you're having dinner with us?" Cookie asked placing her hands on her hips.

"Don't play me." Alicia giggled.

"It doesn't even smell like you started." She said sniffing the air.

"I haven't. I was on the couch reading. But I would love for you to help me if you don't mind." Cookie pouted.

"You can't be serious?" Alicia smacked her lips.

"As a heart attack. Now please." She begged.

"Fine." Cookie beamed with joy.

Her and Alicia hadn't cook together in years. Before Tobias accident, Cookie and Alicia would cook Sunday dinners together every week. But things had changed. And Cookie understood why. So, she was thankful for the given time they shared. The duo moved around the kitchen for two hours. Mixing and dicing. Chopping and blending until it was time for dinner to come out of the oven. "I set the table for the three of us. Is it anything else you need me to do?" Alicia questioned.

"Umm." Cookie examined the kitchen. "No. I think I have it from here. I'm going to take the pie out, and that will be it." Cookie told.

"Ok. Good. I'm going to use the restroom so I could wash up for dinner." Alicia stated.

"Ok." Cookie sang. As Alicia were turning to walk away she glanced back at Cookie one final time.

"God, it makes me so happy to finally see her happy. God bless the man who has her heart." Alicia smiled.

***

"Who car is that?" Chris mumbled when he pulled into Cookie's driveway. He had never seen the Chevy Impala before. "She didn't tell me she was having company today. It better not be one of those male clients, I tell you that." He hissed. Chris climbed out of his car and walked over to the Chevy impala. He typed the tag number into the registration application on his phone and waited for the information to come back.

BEEP.

The notification sounded. "Tobias Smith?" Chris growled. He shoved his phone back in his pocket and raced to the door. He fumbled his keyring for Cookie's house key. He placed it inside the lock and sighed heavily. "What the hell am I doing?" He mumbled. Chris didn't want to blow his cover by revealing he had a key to her place without permission. "Just relax man. All you have to do is go inside and see. It's not like she know you out here." He thought.

Chris placed the keys back in his pocket then took the initiative to knock on the door.

KNOCK. KNOCK.

A minute had passed and there was no answer. Chris was becoming impatient. He reached out and twisted the knob. Surprisingly, the door popped open. Chris could hear Cookie's voice coming from the kitchen. She were singing along to Monica "Everything To Me." Hitting high note after another. Just as Chris was turning the corner, the mystery guest strutted out of the hall bathroom, damn near knocking him over.

"Oh my goodness. I'm sorry." Alicia apologized trying to adjust herself.

"Are you o..."

"Chris?" Alicia whispered frantically. "What are you doing here?" She questioned.

"Oh shit! Think Chris." Chris mind was running a race of it's own.

"Aww. Looks like the two of you have met. I didn't have to even introduce the two of you." Cookie sang proudly as she walked out of the kitchen. "Hello?" Cookie said snapping her fingers.

"Oh, yeah baby. It's a pleasure meeting your friend. You said Alicia, right?" He asked eyeing her sideways.

"That's correct Mr. Kemp." Alicia said emphasizing his name.

"Great! Now that the two of you have met, Alicia you don't have to keep wondering and guessing who he is. What do you think?" Cookie asked putting Alicia on the spot.

"Isn't my honey handsome?" Cookie winked.

"Deadly." Alicia hissed.

"Huh?" Cookie frowned.

"I said indeed." She lied. Chris and Alicia continued staring each other down.

"I knew you'll say that." Cookie smiled.

"So, Chris let's get this straight now. You've met my best friend and she means the world to me. So, know that you have gained a sister. Someone who's been riding with me from day one. I expect you to love her and treat her as such." Cookie explained.

"No problem." Chris grinned. "So, Alicia what kind of work you do?" He smirked. Alicia shook her head.

"I work for some dumb hoe. I've been working for her for quite some time now. The evil bitch just recently got married. I wonder how that's going." Alicia shot back.

"Hopefully good. But who cares?" Cookie shrugged.

"Only the jealous." Chris smirked.

Alicia looked Chris up and down and shook her head in disgust. "Cookie, I think it's time for me to leave. I suddenly lost my appetite." Alicia spat.

"But you didn't even taste the pie I made. Come on, just stay." Cookie begged.

"No, baby. Let her go home and rest. She may need it." Chris assured her.

"Yeah. I do." Alicia said rolling her eyes. She grabbed her purse off the couch and headed for the door.

"Drive safe Alicia. And I hope you're able to keep that job. Just think before you talk out of tone to your boss. Jobs are hard to come by." Chris smiled wickedly.

"And so are good men." Alicia said walking out the door.

"She was nice." Chris lied.

"She's actually a doll. She's just going through a lot. But hey, are you ready to eat?" Cookie asked.

"Yes, baby. And there's something else I want to talk to you about."

"Ok. Go ahead." Cookie said leading him into the kitchen.

"Tomorrow, night I'm having a Banquet for a few of my artist. So, whatever plans we've had for tomorrow, cancel them. I promise I'll make it up to you." He pleaded.

"Ok. No problem. Now sit. Let's eat." She ordered. Cookie placed the different trays of food on the table then joined Chris to devour each entree. After hours of sitting there talking about any and everything, they never made it for there walk on the beach. Instead, they stayed in, and made love all night.

CHAPTER 8

Tonight was the big event. Two of Chris's artist had gone platinum. So, Chris decided to celebrate. Inviting artist from state to state, to make this night one to remember. Tony and Klied were running Chris's label to the best of their ability. The money was pouring in left and right. Klied discovered new talent every week. While Tony kept the label in order. Chris was grateful because all he had to do was sign off on the checks. Other than that, he barely lifted a finger whenever he did stop in to check on things. But tonight was the night. And he was proud of himself and his team. "Baby, I'm going to mingle with Klied and Tony. Will you be ok by yourself until I return?" Chris asked. "Yes baby." Chris kissed her lips and disappeared within the crowd of people. "That man, that man." She thought to herself as she wondered over to the dessert table.

Meanwhile, Stacey one of the platinum artist, were on the other side of the room trying to signal her attention.

"Brittany!" Stacey called out across the room. "Brittany! Over here!" She waved her hand. Still, she couldn't seem to get her attention. So, instead of trying to scream over the music, Stacey made her way over to cake table where Brittany was. "Mrs. Kemp!" Stacey said tapping her on the shoulder. She turned around and smiled. "I was calling your name trying to signal your attention. I figured you didn't hear me being that the music is so loud. I wanted us to take a picture together." Stacey explained.

"Ok. No problem. Let me just wipe these crumbs off my face and refresh my lipstick and I'll be ready to go." Cookie assured.

"Ok. Cool." Stacey smiled. As she were waiting for Brittany to finish getting herself together, her good friend Mya walked up.

"Hey Stacey, girl! Why are you over here standing by yourself?" She asked.

"Actually, I'm not. I'm waiting for Mrs. Kemp to come out of the restroom. As a matter of fact, here she comes now." Stacey nodded.

"Are you ready?" She smiled.

"Yes, but before we head over to the booth, I would like you to meet my good friend Mya. Mya's a upcoming artist. Your husband signed her two weeks ago." Stacey mentioned.

"That's awesome Mya! I know you're excited"

"I really am! I'm thankful for Stacey. If it wasn't for her, I wouldn't have even got this opportunity." She explained

"Brittany, I keep telling her God has a way of doing things. But she doesn't believe me." Stacey explained.

"Yes he does. But Stacey, my name isn't Brittany. My name is Cookie." Stacey frowned.

"Cookie?" She asked with a puzzled look.

"Yes. Cookie." She clarified.

"Hmm. I could've sworn Klied said your name was Brittany." Stacey said trying to reshuffle her thoughts.

"Silly me. I heard wrong." Stacey laughed.

"Good thing I didn't call you Brittany. I would've felt like an ass." Mya chimed in.

"Ladies, it's fine. Now let's get to the picture booth before that crowd swarm in." Cookie said grabbing them both by the arms. The ladies were all smiles as they walked together. All eyes were on them. They commanded everyone's attention. All three ladies were dressed to impress. Their glamorous appearance, spoke volumes.

"I swear I want to marry Mya." Tony said with drooling eyes.

"You can marry whoever you want. As long as you don't touch the one in the middle my brother." Chris stated matter of factly.

BEEP. BEEP.

A text notification sounded.

"Babe, where are you? I've been calling your office and your cell. Wherever you are it's impossible you have reception because my calls are being ignored. If you get this message soon, call me. I'm stuck in the office working. I'll be home no later than two in the morning. No worries, Alicia is here with me.

-Brittany."

After reading the text, Chris didn't bother to respond. His eyes were glued on Cookie. "Excuse me gentlemen. But that beauty is calling my name." He informed. Chris made his way through the crowded room and crept up behind Cookie. There she stood wearing a mahogany colored dress that hugged her curves well. Cookie looked as though she had stepped out of the Ebony magazine. "Do you know, you're the talk of the night?" Chris said whispering in Cookie's ear.

"Well thank you. But please step back. I believe my man is watching me harder than you are." She blushed.

"Is that right?" He played along.

"Yes. He's about six foot two, solid. Handsome fellow. He's wearing a black custom made Versace Tuxedo." She detailed.

"Hmm. That sounds like me." Chris grinned.

"It definitely is baby!" Cookie reached up and planted a wet kiss on his lips.

"I'm ready to get you home." He flirted.

"I know you are. I can feel it through your pants." She winked.

"Let's get out of here and head back to my place. I'll take you home after you catch at least three." He grinned.

"Lead the way baby!" Cookie shouted. Chris didn't mumble another word. Instead he escorted her to his car and drove her straight to his house. "Babe, this house is gorgeous." Cookie admired.

"Thank you." He smiled.

"Hopefully, one day you can move in here with me." He gamed. Cookie blushed and began unbuttoning her dress. "Slow down baby. I have a California King upstairs." He told. He swept Cookie off her feet and carried her inside the house. Instead of retiring to one of the guest bedrooms, he took her to the room he shared with Brittany and laid her down in the bed. He made sweet passionate love to her until the clock struck midnight. "Now you can go home." He winked.

"After all those rounds, I'm ready baby." Cookie giggled.

"Ok. It's so dark in here, let me help you out of the bed. I don't want you to trip on anything." He gamed.

"Just hit the light." Cookie said.

"No need. I got you, baby." Chris was smart. He knew if he would've turned on the light in their bedroom all hell would've broke loose. Brittany had a shelf full of wigs and tonight wasn't the night to explain. So, he escorted Cookie all the way out of the house in the dark.

***

The next morning, Chris made it his business to beat Alicia to work. He knew she was the one who opened and closed Brittany's office, Sunday to Sunday. "Aren't you here bright and early?" Chris spoke sarcastically as Alicia stepped off the elevator.

"That I am! You piece of shit!" She spat harshly. Chris chuckled.

"I'll take that. But I want you to take this. Mind your business Ms. Smith. I don't want to end your career before it even starts. So, before you run and open your mouth to

Brittany or Cookie, please think twice. I'm sure it wouldn't be easy taking care of those two boys without a job." He stated firmly. Alicia's lip quivered. She felt manipulated. She felt defeated. She valued her friendship with Cookie and she needed her job. She couldn't afford to lose it behind Chris's bullshit and games. "Do I make myself clear?" He growled.

"Yes." She hissed. Just as she was turning to walk away Brittany walked in.

"Good morning!" She sang.

"Good morning, babe." Chris smiled cheerfully.

"I thought you were at the label. What are you doing here?" She questioned.

"Ugh...Wanted to see your beautiful face once again. This morning just wasn't enough." He gamed.

GIGGLES.

Brittany and Chris directed their attention over to a chuckling Alicia. "Is there a clown in the room Ms. Smith?" Brittany asked. Alicia looked back at Chris and down at her desk.

"Yes! Your fucking husband!" She spat.

"Excuse me bitch!" Brittany barked.

"You heard me! And he feel me too! I fucking quit!" Alicia growled. She grabbed her purse and the few pictures of Torrent off her desk and brushed passed the two of them.

"When you dot that elevator, your black ass better not circle back!" Brittany yelled at her back. Alicia immediately stopped in her tracks and glanced over her shoulder.

"You need to dot your husband. Bitch!" Alicia smirked. She entered the waiting elevator and turned around with the biggest smile across her face.

"What the hell is she talking about Chris?" Brittany huffed.

"Who knows? I don't even know the crazy chick." Chris lied.

"You got crazy right!" Brittany sighed heavily.

"Baby, don't let her work your nerves. Let's just go home and close things down for the day." Chris instructed.

"No. I can't baby. A lot has to be done around here. I can't let that miserable bitch fuck up my day. And besides, my employees will be coming in, in an hour." She said looking down at her watch.

"Brittany, that wasn't a question. It was an order. You will not lose my son behind stress. Now lock up the damn office, power off your cellphone for the remainder of the day and get your ass home! Now!" He ordered. Brittany's eyes widen.

"Ok." She whispered frantically. She quickly wrote a note on a sheet of white paper and taped it to the door. In a timely manner, she locked up the office and was in route home with Chris on her trail. When they arrived home, they both retired to their joined bedroom.

"Do you need anything baby?" Chris asked.

"No. I'm just going to lay down and rest." She assured him.

"Ok. I'll be on the balcony." He stated.

"Wait. What's this?" She asked.

"What baby?" He questioned.

"This. A strain of hair. Burgundy hair at that!" She frowned. Chris heart began fluttering. He knew exactly where it came from. Cookie's name was written all over it.

"I better ask Cieon. She's the one changed the linens. Maybe her hair got caught up in the sheets." He lied.

"You're right. Send her a text and let her know please." Brittany told.

"I'm on it now. Just get rest." He said making his way outside. "Damn that was close." He sighed. "All these lies are starting to catch up with my ass.

CHAPTER 9

Alicia sat in her car with a soul full of tears and a heart full of hurt. She wanted nothing but the best for Cookie. She had been hurt so many times and no matter what age group or race she targeted it was the same old sad love song. "You have to tell her." Alicia tried convincing herself. But it wasn't working. "I can't. I can't!" Alicia was right. She couldn't. It would have hurt Cookie even more knowing she knew the entire time. "Come on. Think!" Alicia said clenching her fist. She shuffled her thoughts and came up short until a Facebook notification sounded on her phone. "I got it!" She yelled.

Alicia quickly created a fake Facebook account. She visited Brittany's profile and captured screenshots of her and Chris's wedding photos and different family pictures. She searched for Cookie's page, then sent her the photos and a simple message. *"Sorry, to be the barrier of bad news but he's NO GOOD."*

***

All afternoon roses of every color had been delivered to Cookie's house from Chris. Big boxes, small boxes, you name it. Each gift was different. Some were clothes, some were jewelry, even a box that held two thousand dollars. "Wow." Cookie smiled from ear to ear. She couldn't believe her eyes. Her doorbell sounded for a hour straight. It felt like Christmas. "I better call and tell him I received the gifts." She beamed with joy. As she retrieved her phone from the tabletop, a social media notification came in. "What is this?" Cookie's happy moment faded. Her smile had flipped upside down. "This can't be true. This can't be real." Cookie choked on her words as she stared at the phone. "This the same woman who was at the label that day." A shocking look plastered her face. "I have to call him!" She sobbed. Just as she began dialing on the keypad, a knock came at the door. *KNOCK. KNOCK.*

Cookie looked up from the phone and over at the door. "This bastard has the audacity to show up at my house!" She raged. She rushed to the door and pulled it open. "You son of a..." It wasn't Chris.

"Did I come at a bad time?" Tony questioned.

"No! You came at the perfect fucking time!" She shouted.

"What did I do?" He nervously asked.

"Bring your narrow ass inside and see for yourself!" Cookie stormed over to the counter. Rushing to get her phone. She was trembling so bad, she could barely grip it. "Explain this!" She said dangling the phone in his face. Tony dropped his head when he realized what appeared on the screen. "Tony, please don't lie to me. Just be honest." Cookie begged. Tony shook his head.

"Cookie, I can't get involved in that." He said.

"Tony, please! My heart is heavy right now! I've placed my trust into this man and this is what I get. I'm parading around the banquet, smiling and grinning as though I'm "The Mrs. Kemp" and the entire time this bastard had a whole wife at home!" Cookie raged.

"Cookie what do you expect me to say? I love you like a sister and always will. I've always given you the upmost respect! But you can't expect me to overstep my boundaries and tell you what's going on when it's not my place!" Tony tried to reason.

"Save the bullshit and get out of my house! Now!" Cookie barked. Tony shook his head. He threw his hands up and walked out of the house. Tears streamed down Cookie's face. Not only was she losing a man who she thought was the world, but a true friend who she looked to as a brother.

***

Cookie sat at her kitchen table drinking a glass a wine trying to calm her nerves. She had called Chris phone several times, but her calls were left unanswered. "I can't sit here any longer. I have to go find this bitch!" She hissed. Just as Cookie stood up, the door opened.

"So, you didn't see me calling your phone?" Chris snapped.

"Of course I did! I even seen your wife and child on Facebook!" Cookie yelled. Quietness filled the air. "Wow, so you have nothing to say?" Cookie barked.

"No matter what I say, you're not going to believe it anyway. So, why even bother." Chris said trying to flip the script.

"Cut the bullshit Chris! Now it makes sense why your artist kept calling me Brittany. And it explains why you crawl your ass out of my bed six o'clock every morning!" She spat.

"What do you want me to say Brittany!" In that moment, he had wished those words wouldn't have left his lips.

"Brittany?" Cookie smirked. "You called me your wife name? Really?" She barked. "I tell you what, get the fuck out and stay out! Leave now before I shoot!" Cookie rushed up her cabinet in search of the twenty two she had stashed away. Chris, knew what she was going to get, so without further ado, he left. "God why this is happening to me? Why?" Cookie cried as she held on to the table for support. She felt her legs would give out at any given moment. "Please help me God." She begged. Cookie slid to the floor, and prayed until she fell asleep in that same spot.

CHAPTER 10

SNAP. CLICK.

Chris's camera sounded. He sat across the street from Cookie's house snapping pictures of her house, the cars that rested in her yard, and the company that had just came over for a visit. "How can she move on like this!" He spat as he bit down on the candy sneaker bar. "I was good her! I loved her!" He hissed. "This nigga isn't going to win like this! I'll put up a hell of a fight first!" He growled. Chris climbed out of his car wearing an all-black hoodie and black jeans.

Luckily, it was dark outside. So, it made it easier for him to blend in with the darkness. Chris quickly crept into Cookie's yard. Ducking down behind Cookie's male friend car. "Dumb nigga!" He barked. Chris reached in his pocket and grabbed two sneaker bars. He unwrapped them both placing one bar into the guy gas tank and the other in

Cookie's. "Checkmate." He laughed hysterically as he walked towards the house to finish what he was about to start.

***

Months had passed and the calls and texts had finally stop. Chris had finally gotten the picture. She started seeing a guy name Jason. Jason was laid back kind of guy. He was honest and sweet. But he wasn't Chris. Cookie found herself missing Chris at times but she had to let him go. "Sweetheart, is everything ok?" Jason asked snapping her out of her thoughts.

"Yes." Cookie whispered.

"You haven't touched your food. And I was asking you what day would you like to fly to Bahamas." He told.

"I'm sorry. I...I...have a lot on my mind. Please forgive me." She explained.

"It's fine. I'm aware that you are stressed about something. I see it all in your face." He started. "So, allow me to remove this tray from your lap and get you a little comfortable.

"Ok." Cookie blushed. Jason placed the try on the dresser and walked back over to Cookie.

"Come sit on the edge of the bed." He said tapping the spot. "I'm going to massage your shoulders and sing you a song. How does that sound?" He asked.

"Relaxing." Cookie smiled. Jason helped her peel the peach robe off her shoulders then he placed his masculine hands on her and began caressing her slowly.

***

"Look at this shit!" Chris spat. "She got another nigga in our house. Rubbing on the body that supposed to belong to me!" He barked. Chris had pulled a ladder from behind the bushes, extending up Cookie's bedroom balcony.

With the ladder's help, Chris had a full view of everything. "These motherfuckers playing a dangerous game!" He growled. "But I have something for that. Chris climbed back off the ladder and crept over to her flower garden. What can I use?" He mumbled as his eyes scanned the area. "Bingo." He grinned wickedly. His eyes landed on the concrete stepping stones. "This should be good." He laughed hysterically.

***

BOOM.

"Oh shit! What was that!" Cookie jumped.

"I'm not sure! Sound like it came from downstairs. Stay here, let me go find out." Jason instructed.

"No! I'm coming with you." Cookie stated firmly.

"Fine. But just stay close behind me." Jason opened the bedroom door and peaked his head out. He looked back at Cookie and shook his head. He placed his index finger up to his lips, signaling her to remain quiet. Jason peaked over the staircase looking down at the foyer. He didn't see anything. And he didn't hear a sound. He reached for Cookie's hand and the two quietly eased down the staircase. When the two turned the corner that's when they saw the damage.

"What in the hell!" Cookie screamed. Shattered glass was everywhere. And the stone that helped break the glass rested in the middle of her floor.

"Call the police!" Jason ordered. Just as Cookie reached for the phone, a loud nose came rattling through the door.

BAM! BOOM!

Chris had a hammer in his hand banging and beating on the doorknob. "Who is that?" Jason yelled.

"Come to the door and find out nigga!" It was Chris. Cookie shook her head in despair.

"It's Chris. My ex." Cookie whispered frantically.

BOOM.

"What is he doing here!" Jason questioned.

"Who knows. But I have to get you out of here." Cookie whispered. Jason frowned.

"I'm not scared Cookie. Let me go handle this like a man!" Jason stated firmly.

"No. I can't. Just please, let me distract him. Leave through the back. I don't want any problems! Please do it for me. Please!" Cookie begged.

BOOM. BAM.

Jason looked at the door and back over at Cookie. "Fine. But lose my number and get your shit together." Jason hissed. He jogged to the back door and let himself out of the shattered glass sliding door. Cookie quickly grabbed her cell off the counter and opened the screen. Four picture messages had come in from Chris earlier that evening.

"Oh my goodness. He's been watching us." Cookie's chest heaved up and down. She closed the messages and called Tony. "Tony, it's Cookie. Please get over here now! Chris has completely gone crazy!" She yelled into this phone. She disconnected the call and tossed the phone back on the counter.

BOOM. BAM.

Just as Cookie was walking towards the front door, it came tumbling off the hinges. "Where the fuck is he!" Chris spat harshly.

"He's not here! Please stop Chris! Please!" She begged.

"I'm not stopping shit! Who was that nigga!" He barked.

"Chris please. Just go! It doesn't matter. He's not here. Go home to your wife!" She pleaded as tears streamed down her cheeks.

"I'm not going to tell you again! You have two minutes to answer me! Or I'm going to burn this house down!" He warned.

"Please!" Cookie shook tremendously.

"I'm...I'm...pregnant!" She cried. In that moment everything froze; time, Cookie, and Chris.

"You what?" Chris spat.

"Yeah man. She is. Just let her go big dawg. You've done enough." Tony said rushing through the door. Chris looked at Tony and back at Cookie. She were shaking as though it was below twenty degrees.

"I'm sorry." Chris mouthed. Cookie broke into a loud cry and ran up the stairs. Just as Chris started behind her, Tony grabbed his arm.

"Let her go big dawg. Enough has been done." He told.

"I fucked up!" Chris hissed. "I fucked up!" He punched the wall. "She'll never forgive me!" He roared.

"Chris, you have to do better. You can't do this. And I can't do this. I'm stuck between a disaster you created. Just allow Cookie to live her life and be happy. Let her move on. Just take care of your seed when it comes. Bro distant yourself before you lose everything." Tony tried to reason.

"I'm afraid I can't do that." Chris shrugged.

"And why is that man? Look around at the damage you've caused. You could've went to jail tonight." Tony yelled.

"Tony, I'm a man that loves it all. I love my life, I love my wife. And I love Cookie. Cookies are desserts. Everyone loves desserts. They're so good you just can't get enough of them. So, I'm going to have my cake and ice cream and I'm going to eat it too."

EPILOGUE

I guess you guys looking at me as though I'm the bad guy now. But how can you judge this book by its title? I love Brittany and I love Cookie too. Sometimes it's hard to choose between the one you've married and the one you wish you would've met first. They both are good women. And I can't choose between the two. It's impossible. My heart lies in both their hands. I did what I could do by telling you all my side. To you, it was based on all my lies. But hey everybody has a story to tell. And I guess now Brittany is ready to share her side being that she feels I didn't tell it all. So, sit back and let's wait to hear how her story unfolds...

Made in the USA
Columbia, SC
29 August 2019